HALAL PORK
AND OTHER STORIES

 UpSet Press, Inc.
P.O. Box 200340
Brooklyn, NY 11220
www.upsetpress.org

UpSet Press is an independent, not-for-profit, tax-exempt (501c3) small press based in Brooklyn, New York. The mission of the press is to support and showcase innovative and progressive work by emerging writers (first/second books), as well as to restore to print rare and out-of-print works (again with a special focus on first/second books). Founded in 2000 by a group of Brooklyn-based poets, the press intends to publish one to two books annually. In addition to its publishing endeavors, the press conducts regular poetry workshops and readings around New York City.

Library of Congress Control Number: 2010941234

First printing, March, 2011
ISBN 978-0-9760142-3-2
Printed in the United States
10 9 8 7 6 5 4 3 2 1

Dedicated to Chowder Jackson, illegitimate stepchild of Joe Jackson father of the Jackson5, thrown into the alligator swamps in 1979.

Had he lived, this book would not need to have been written.

TABLE OF CONTENTS

AUTHOR'S NOTE

As of the publishing of this book, there is no such thing as Halal Pork. If there was, the implication would be that the East and West, with all their differences of opinion, would have reconciled over a feta cheese breakfast and a smoothie. Talk about ambitious. The combination makes fundies (fundamentalists, not to be confused with mentalists who just have extreme thoughts without the fun) squeal, moderates gawk and the so-called infidels, "say what?" Kevin Bacon is inherently pork but Omar Bacon is Halal Pork. Two Muslim girls in hijab go clothes shopping. Hijab, not to be confused with the Burqa, only covers the hair allowing for all types of secular adornments from uggz to rainbow fat laces while still staying modest aka halal. They find a dress perfect in one sense but realize the sequence lettering "Slut Grrll!" inscribed on the buttock area is going over the top. They say the dress is Halal Pork. After all, it doesn't have to stricty refer to food or rather halal ham, which would be like ordering a fatwa sandwich with a side of be-headcheese. Now that's unacceptable, after all, no one likes floating mystery meat in gelatin. America, as the Italian Cartographer who named it would say, is a country in transition with a case of Aytch Pee (pheonetic of H.P or see title of book). People say: You're the missing link Cihan, what made you write this?

And I say: I wish it was a summer job with vacation but it started pretty awful and continues to remind me of my mortality on a near minute-by-minute replay.

It's been barrels of fun and it continues as the living landbridger can testify. Amen, shalom, salaam, Shanti.

THE CRIMEAN SALADIN

Mehmet Vatanoglu's (pronounced vah-tan-O-loo) real name was Mustafa Patrov. His tie was a blend of polyester and rayon, the poor man's silk. Poly rayon, although being a popular substitute for silk, actually feels nothing like the real thing. Mustafa, or rather Mehmet, adjusted the new tie, proud of his reflection. His mother had told him back in the homeland, "A man's tie reflects his soul." To that effect, Mustafa, or rather Mehmet, reflected a Tatar displaced from a homeland, now living in Brooklyn, and wearing a silk rip-off. He brushed the dust from his overstarched shirt and threw on the corduroy blazer he usurped from the local thrift store. We say "usurped" here to differentiate between the slight act Mustafa committed the day before (in order to get the suit) and the part of the world Mustafa is actually from, which we shall refer to as "stolen," since it was stolen from the Tatars, incidentally and more specifically the Crimean Tatars, by the Russians way back in 1944.

Crimea, or *Kirim*, or *Qirim*, depending on which side of it you're from, is a little known isthmus in the Black Sea. It is also, ironically, the point of origin for the remaining Crimean Tatars on the planet, spread out like a frugal smear of tartar sauce over a globalized fried fish fillet. Mehmet thought of his people and their cause. He thought of the search for a stolen homeland and their right to return. Mehmet thought about all the things that come with being displaced and left his house as Mustafa, Savior of the Tatary.

This new identity served to keep him focused and on track towards the eventual goal of all goals, the great meaning to life, and solution for any poet living in a capitalist world—to buy back his stolen homeland, one acre at a time. The idea was actually given to him by Erik Estrada, star of the hit seventies cop show, *C.H.I.P.'s*. Estrada appeared on a late night infomercial asking for investments in pre-construction opportunities in Mississippi swampland. "Invest now and see a huge return on your investment once the tourists start coming to the future: Mississippi Techburb, an ideal world of suburbs and Midwest charm meets Silicon Alley and SoHo."

"Great idea," Mehmet thought. "If a C-list actor can sell swampland based on its Midwest charm, I can sell Kirim for the same!" Finally, a tangible idea could be applied to Crimea, or rather the dream of it. The dream was of the Golden Khanate, complete with Sultans and Grand Viziers and mosques inlaid with grape vines surrounded by happy people. All of them Crimean Tatar, of course, and none of them Russian, seeing as how the Russians seized the land officially fifteen minutes after giving Tatar families a knock at their doors at four in the morning. It was another case of, "Wake up! Get the fuck out and die on these train cars waiting for you!"

Near the end of World War II, the Tatar inhabitants were put on boundless freight trains where most died of starvation and inhumane circumstances, particularly being in train cars for over forty days without food, water, or sanitation. Others were put on boats that were placed in the middle of the sea and sunk. Pregnant women delivered stillborn fetuses due to lack of much of anything on the train cars. Groups of young Tatar boys were massacred for made-up accusations of working with the Germans. The Crimean Genocide was the last move of a 200–year push to take Crimea, which had started with Catherine the Great, who referred to the isthmus as "the only place on Earth that resembles heaven." As far as genocides go, the Crimean one was essentially successful, which is why most people are unaware of it. Go figure. Tatars can only track back one generation now, like androids implanted with thought memories. Thus, you have displaced Tatars, now citizens of whatever country they landed in, escaped to, or otherwise ended up in, thinking they have no past, or some seriously imagined one. More recently, the Crimea has been home to Russian vacationers and young rich Europeans looking for a weekend to create their own memories—without the Tatars, of course. Mehmet, literally the Last of the Mohicans, or in this case the Last of the Tauri, upon realizing that his homeland was being devoured by Russo-hipsters in search of naked dance parties, changed his name and "usurped" the new suit. Erik Estrada gave him the meaning to life.

The first suit was brown corduroy because to him, the jagged smoothness of the fabric's striated pattern spoke of dynamism and style. If Calvin Klein had a say in it, he would call it Tatar-chic, the new Scythian fashion confab. Little did he know the actual effects of corduroy on social interactions in the twenty-first century. Perhaps his first misstep, he decided his new suit should be distinctive to make him appear important to his community of Crimean Tatars in Brooklyn. This distinction would give him a platform for his new real estate revolutionaries ASAP.

A cluster of bodies in paperboy hats, corduroy, denim, and polyester stood on the corner of Kings Highway. They were recent to not-so-recent immigrants waiting in front of a door on an old brick building, above which was this misspelled sign: *Asimilation Service: Reports, Greencurd, Divorce, Emploiment.* The director of A.S. was a certain somebody with enough smarts to know that volume is the key to profit. Mehmet stood indifferently; last in a line of immigrants ready to spend their last borrowed dollars on becoming a quick American. Mehmet noticed a man climbing up the fire escape, assumingly locked out of his apartment.

"*Yalanji!*" the man yelled, a Turkish expression tantamount to "liar of lies" or "the worst kind of liar." Turkish, it can be argued, is the common derivative language of most Central Asians, who oddly enough blame the Uzbeks for this. We will perform translations for the reader from here on, assuming an English-Turkic short story would have a limited reader base and probably be accused of insulting the other half of the hyphen.

"Altan *bey*!" Mehmet said.

"You're a liar, Mehmet. Hold on, I'm coming down," said the Kazak on the fire escape. Looking at his watch, Mehmet grimaced, then returned to a more plastic smile.

The Kazak dropped down and approached him. "$60,000?"

"Yes, what about it?"

"You took my grandmother for $60,000?! You dirty son-of-a-whore!"

"Calm down, Altan. This is going to a good cause!"

"I heard all about your little fantasy. You're a liar, a hustler, and—"

"Brother, brother, look at me. Don't you see this jacket?"

"What about it?" said the Kazak.

"I'm serious. This is not a joke! We're going to build a huge multiplex hotel, mall, movie theater..."

The Kazak stared at the corduroy brown illumination. "Nice blazer."

"Right, I'm not joking. The Russians will be eating out of our hands in no time." Mehmet spent the greater part of the first month visiting local Crimean Tatars and pitching the idea after receiving what he called "The Inspiration." They were skeptical at first, but a $1,000 investment turned into $10,000 and so on. Each time he pitched the idea, it got more convincing and concise until eventually he had his pitch down pat. Mehmet had mastered the American art of the sale in his own way.

A newly shaved Mustafa, or rather Mehmet, sat across from the Beyenoglus, an older Tatar couple whose kids had been married off and whose memories of homeland permeated their modest Queens apartment. A portrait of a random scene from ancient Tatary hung prominently above the sofa they sat on. Altan Beyenoglu, a man of staunch character and thick eyebrows, leaned towards the salesman. "Mehmet *bey*, your plan sounds like a fantasy. We live modest lives here, and the Russians will not let Kirim go. We have seen this over and over again since 1944."

Altan's wife interceded, "Yes, you can buy all the land in the world, still the mafia will take it from up under you and we Tatars will just sit there, taking whatever the Russians give us or take away!"

"Dear, let's not get into a political discussion. We cannot fight for Kirim. We are not Palestinians." Altan reached for his cigarettes, readying himself for the millionth political debate with his wife today. "Tatars are a proud people. Do they expect a fight to come out from us? We have no will to fight them."

Without hesitation, Mehmet recognized the couple's abysmal outlook and brightened up, as if feeding off the void. "In the twenty-first century, we don't fight for land, we buy it! If the Palestinians had any sense they would get the richest ones to build attractions—spectacles, that if destroyed—"

"Mehmet *bey*, I understand. If you were Palestinian I would debate you on this, but their problems are not equal to the Tatars. We were successfully wiped off the map. We have no voice, no homeland."

"Altan *abi*," Mehmet spoke sincerely, referring to the older man in the formal *abi*, a Turkish extension to indicate elder brother, "why do you think you do not exist? You are here. I am here. I am doing something and trying. How can you say you don't exist?"

The old man looked deeply into his wife's eyes. Eyes that had seen the train cars, execution squads, and drownings; eyes that witnessed her own still-born two weeks after being forced onto the aimless routes around southern Russia, subsequently having to dispose of the dead fetus herself tossing it off the train somewhere in Uzbekistan. Most importantly her eyes remembered what Kirim was before the Russians, before the Germans, before the accusations and famines, when exotic grapes grew in Bakhchisaray decorated by the history of the Khans and architecture of the Golden Khanate.

"Say we give you the $1,000 you ask for. What is the guarantee of a return?"

"Don't look for a financial return, Altan *abi*," Mehmet said with a childlike splendor, "Look for a permanent return—to your *vatan*."

Vatan is an important concept for a Tatar, as it not only translates to homeland, but to "*the* homeland." So *vatan* is always Kirim—not Queens, not Sydney, not anywhere the remaining point five percent of the diaspora have settled.

Mehmet got the investment capital remarkably, and each time his pitch refined itself more and more. The diaspora would insist it was a useless cause and enter a fatalistic mode. As soon as their eyes glazed over with loss, Mustafa would turn into Mehmet, the sales hawk, and strike at any pessimism rising to the occasion by offering the dream. Pessimism is, after all, the playground for failure.

Regep Adnan, owner of *Çibörek Delight*, was a lonely Tatar, his darling wife having passed away of natural causes. All he had was his store, the local Central Asian "bread and olive" store. Regep had no next of kin, no living family and nowhere to place the money he had made. That is, until Mehmet came to the store and pitched his pre-construction opportunities in the Crimea.

"I can tell you right now the cost of land, since the Soviet collapse, is increasing ten percent every year." He pounded the table between the shop owner and him.

Regep flinched at the motion.

"Regep *bey*, this means if you bought a parcel of Crimea in 1994 for $10,000, it would now be worth one million."

Regep leaned back with thick white mustache in hand, doing the calculations. "Your math is all wrong, my friend."

"Okay, well, perhaps it is," Mehmet conceded, fixing his new burgundy corduroy blazer, purchased courtesy of his donations.

The immediacy of his concession seemed odd to Regep, who replied, "Plus the only way to get back home is to fight our way."

Mehmet looked at Regep, felt the tiger spirit of the salesman rising, and sealed the deal.

"Freedom and *vatan*," Mehmet recited in a near heroic final call, "is bought not fought."

Regep wasn't biting. He was suspicious. "Your catchphrases are indeed catchy Mehmet. If freedom is bought then why—"

Mehmet ignored the doubt just thrown at him and looked at his reflection on the handle of a spoon inside a bucket of pickled vegetables. The spoon distorted his body, making him look like a reflection in a funhouse mirror. Like a tape loop he interrupted, "Feel good about resting in peace in your homeland, where you have always belonged. Die loved."

"Die loved? By whom? My wife is dead and I have no family. So tell me again brother, who will love me when I die if I die in Kirim?"

Mehmet was stunned. Up until this moment, most of his "leads" took him for face value.

"I am Mehmet Vatanoglu."

"Vatan—Oglu. Vatan—Oglu," Regep repeated as if separating the syllables would reveal some hidden truth. "Who was your father, Mehmet?"

"I don't think my personal life concerns the issue of our return to Kirim, sir."

"Forgive me in advance, but you come into my place of business with huge claims of me being loved during death. Are you not concerned about being seen as morbid?"

Mehmet, or rather Mustafa, found himself in an awkward position. Among the New York Tatar diaspora he was able to create this believable character to fund his plan except for this shop owner. He didn't need Regep's money. Enough money was saved to actually get the plan off the ground, at least in theory. However, the fabricated Mehmet has gotten the better of the real Mustafa, and we can guess that the almighty spirit of greed was playing a role now. His catchphrases began to show a tinge of the same fatalism he was exploiting.

Regep continued, "Your points are actually so morbid they can be interpreted as being near threatening."

"Sorry for wasting your time." Mehmet, speechless and unable to crawl out of this, headed for the exit.

Regep stopped him. "The Vatanoglus are known for birthmarks on their faces."

Mehmet, or rather Mustafa, stopped dead in his tracks—caught.

"You should have done your research before you decided to act like the Crimean Saladin."

Regep leaned into a barrel of dried chickpeas, a Turkish treat known as *leblebi*, and dropped a handful in his mouth, waiting for the salesman to respond.

Mehmet pulled the door open. His reflection distorted in the glass. He paused.

The shop owner jerked his chin, a very Mediterranean gesture, and shouted, "Who are you?"

He was Mustafa Patrov at one point, another anonymous immigrant in the muck, a short and stout young man, probably in his late thirties. He was a man who decided to identify himself in the plural and do his part in the evolution of a new myth.

"I'm the bastard son of Ataturk, the shunned cousin of Genghis. I am the side of you that has rotted in memories," Mehmet turned towards the lonely shop owner, "only to be resurrected in my arteries! If that will be all, I would like to get on with my business of making us the proud people we were, sir."

Mehmet never left the store. Regep, after hearing the salesman's eulogy, gave up nearly thirty percent of his savings to the cause, that of the great Crimean return and the possibility of owning homeland once and for all. His home brewed contracts were simple and to the point:

I_____ (insert name here) under the authority of Mehmet Vatanoglu (for hereon known as Captain Kirim Associates Ltd) give _____ (said amount of money) to pre-construction opportunities on the Crimean Peninsula now inhabited by lawless Muscovite bullies. I _____ (insert name here) understand that these opportunities may consist of a hotel, a condominium complex, or a New York style pizzeria. Under the terms of this contract it shall be known that _____ (insert percentage) of all land purchased will belong to_____ (insert name here) after the investment has returned its loss and bloomed a new Vatan.

Signed _____(insert name here)
Witness _____(Captain Kirim Associates)

Vatanoglu's assessment of the situation in Crimea had all the ingredients of purpose with a dash of highly enriched food coloring. His persistent efforts led to the fattening of both his bank account and his wardrobe, which in itself is a measure of a man's success to many mothers and parenting magazines. Not only did he have more than one corduroy blazer, he acquired a vast collection of red velvet paintings of dogs playing poker and a Segway personal transporter, decorated with glyphs of Genghis Khan and Timurlane. All this in a year of fabricating the plan to resell Crimea to its original displaced, voiceless inhabitants. Amazing! The power of selling dreams led to material gain. It made sense. Sell a dream to sleepers and use the profit for your own dream while they sleep—or so Mustafa, or rather Mehmet, thought.

These are sensitive times and even more sensitive are the minds in the skulls of the sellers of dreams. The time it took to get investors and inject his catchphrases of purchasing freedom and being buried in the land of your ancestors monopolized much of Mehmet's critical thinking. He even may have glossed over the hard realities many families had endured and could possibly be accused of not considering all the aspects of his plan; for instance, the fact that he had never actually been to Crimea.

"Come to the boat!" called the Captain.

Mehmet, or rather Mustafa, thought, "I am going to drown! Who is this captain? I am the Captain, the leader of my people!"

"Steady now! All aboard!" said the Captain undocking the small ferry. Mehmet, or rather Mustafa, had arrived in Istanbul the day before and took an exhaustive bus ride to the departure port for Crimea in Northern Turkey carrying only a very large suitcase. The bus was crowded and he crouched in a corner, being crushed by an array of diverse travelers from Germany, Russia, and Alpha Centauri in their nationally mandated Star Trek–like silver/red suits (the old Ukraine was now run by a totalitarian sci-fi fan, Pablo Escobaritov). Mehmet wore the corduroy blazer he usurped one year earlier and did everything he could to hide his newly encrusted mouth of gold teeth. He hardly smiled, except at the woman with her farm of sad looking chickens labeled, "*Yeme! Bu kushlar cok hasta,*" which translates from Turkish, "Do not eat. These birds are very sick."

Tatars historically have been generalized as barbarians, even borderline cannibals bent on invading Muscovitian land (see Conan the Barbarian in Cimmeria, texts burned by crusading *Homo gigantus* in 4,000 B.C. [refer to the super-conscious ether that holds our collective intelligence together, location 23-19.17-0x80; or any modern Russian textbook on the subject]). As for himself, Mehmet, or rather Mustafa, had a romanticized idea of Tatar history filled with royal Sultans overseeing vast empires of mosques, silks, and the songs of mystical Muezzins. The reality was more likely a reconciliation of a Central Asian warrior and a Persian poet having small talk over feta cheese and vodka.

"One second!" yelled Mehmet, or rather Mustafa, who opened his suitcase and began to undress.

The Captain yelled back, "Now listen boy, the waters are getting rougher by the second. We have to head out or we're staying here the night!" The passengers yelled at the Captain not to wait any longer.

Out of the suitcase came an outfit in six parts: the Sultan's turban, the elaborate *janassari clothing*, the seal of the Khanate, pointy gypsy shoes, and a stick-on mustache. All of which Mustafa threw on himself before leaping onto the boat to the embarking ship.

"Onward to *Vatan!*" he yelled, pointing at the cloudy and rough waters of a particularly bad day in the Black Sea. The boat shook. Salty waters crashed against the sides.

"Can you believe this water?!" said a woman dressed in a silver/red Star Trek suit, obviously a post-Ukrainian Alpha Centaurian. Mustafa avoided looking at anyone and stood motionless, like the icon he thought he was, and pointed out towards the ocean. The ship rocked and in so doing forced Mehmet, or rather Mustafa, to lose his balance. He crouched down attempting to recover, spreading his hands and waving around, his fake mustache dangling from his lips, his gold teeth exposed by a cringing face. The passengers were unmoved, having all strapped in prior to departure.

At last, Mehmet got his footing and rose again, looking around and feeling for his turban, his teeth, and his mustache. "What's wrong with you people?" he yelled gripping the boats side. "I am here to save you! Control the ship!"

The ship rocked again and with such force that Mehmet, or rather Mustafa, lost his balance for a final time. Much to the dismay of many an investor, the savior of the Tatary, the Crimean Saladin went under, horribly, suffocating in the abysmal waters on the outskirts of a lost paradise.

MISILI MIDHIB, PUNK ROCK HIJABI
FROM ANOTHER DIMENSION

The day Jamil Makam decided to do a 1,500–word story on an up-and-coming Muslim musician, a meteor fell from the sky. A nameless lightning bolt hit a magical Afghan carpet from a distant star, carrying on it a wandering babushka caught in a world between the skies. Drifting space rocks, a homeland memory dropped her through our atmosphere and onto the Central Asian steppe of Coney Island. She walked the rustic shores, lived in broken amusement parks, and worked silently in sideshows.

Her name was an intonation of the larynx and flip of the lip, nearly incoherent by our human tongue but sounding close to *Masaly* or *Misoul-E*. She came to be known by the underbelly of New York exiles as Misili Midhib.

Misili was discovered by sideshow gals known as the Brooklyn Exiles, a group of native New York girls pushed out of their neighborhoods by the hordes of out-of-state kids who now occupied the surrounding lands. They lived communally under the remaining portion of the Coney Island boardwalk. All of them possessed an athleticism that was beyond the masses, which allowed them to do things like swallow swords, hang from ropes using their teeth, and tame snakes with bare hands. The amusement park had been demolished and replaced by a mega-development of condominiums alongside so-called futuristic rides, flashing holograms of explosions, blasting Euro-trance all to entertain the new immigrants (suburban middle American fodder); and the Brooklyn Exiles made their livelihood by performing at the sideshow, the last vestige of the original spirit of the island.

One night, Misili was on break in the dressing room while a fire-eating Suicide Girl from Old Williamsburg juggled for an audience of idiots. Misili's face remained unknown since she never took off the glowing garb she had on.

During these early days, not even her eyes were visible to the outside world. Having abilities beyond human perception, Misili Midhib was able to navigate via emotions and thought-bouncing. As she stood there in that dressing room on that fateful night in Coney Island, the ultimate truth revealed itself to her. The meaning behind meaning…

Misili, the girl from another planet, who walked out on stage dressed in a space suit every night and whirled until she floated, decided to drop the act.

Come watch Coney Island's own Alien Girl, boasted the signs in front.

She turned to the mirror, surrounded by lights and picked up an inch of her head covering. Her cosmic skin was uncovered and it reflected back in the mirror, revealing a girl, a mission, a pure light. It was a knowledge that pulled her deeper underground, performing in subways and fighting to wear her cosmic *hijab* in dive bars and shelters where the New York exiles suffered.

Misili, the girl from another planet. Misili, the bitch with the *hijab*. Misili, the prophetess.

Jamil was too late. Fresh out of school, he worked at the *Innovations for Progressive Islam*, a newsletter. By the time he was able to write his article, Misili was long deceased. The cause—a certain Madame Ayanda Shiraz, the world's premiere French Moroccan writer who now screams in a crazy house her confessions of the murder of Misili Midhib. Confined to her quarters, Shiraz spends these, her later years, in a gloomy dementia.

Jamil sits with her. The year is 2044 and the walls are electronic glass, transparent yet at the same time displaying broadcast images of wars and media overload. Occasionally, a smiling female face appears reminding the two how much time was left for the interview.

"How did you come to know Misli?" he asked.

"*Mis-E-Lee.* Learn to pronounce it right first. I killed that thing," the wretched lady whispered, curled up in her wheelchair, tubes everywhere, staring vacantly at the man with the notepad in front of her.

"I took her under my wing, you see, and she vulgarized me. That thing!"

As a Muslim woman in a post-apocalyptic world obsessed with everything bad about Islam, Shiraz's first book was a wild success. She had etched her role in American society as the representative for Arab female-kind. After writing several more books, Shiraz found herself cornered. Having written only about her alleged victimhood under Islam (*99 Names of the Hornet's Nest, Not Without My Freedom*, and *Allah Forbid*) she literally bound herself inside of it. Of course, Ivy League universities and feminist foundations encouraged her to unveil this oppressive religion responsible for "so much destruction," as Laura Tienam, *Playboy* bunny turned academic feminist, told her. She had become so outspoken on how terrible Muslims were that innumerable *fatwas* were placed on her head by the Muslim right. None of them took shape, especially after the Global Islamic Revolution of 2018.

Ayanda Shiraz became ideologically bankrupt and alone. Miserably busy with parties and supposed research, she devolved into a shell of a writer stuck in her own idea of what her readers wanted; anything that demeaned Islam and made Western religion and culture look better. She ceased to ask herself if any of her fabricated accounts of stoning in the mosque and blood-letting by evil Sheikhs were true (none of them were); that is, until the meteorite struck Coney Island on the last year of the Mayan Calendar, 2012.

Misili strummed the first note of the night on the platform of the West 4th Street train station. She stood at five foot one, a tiny thing wrapped in a futuristic garb echoing a distant star in some alternative dimension. Her bizarre presence and voice mesmerized the commuters as she began to sing, playing what seemed to be a Speak 'n Spell modified with wires and a small speaker:

> *Somewhere between the rocks*
> *and the hard places in between...*

By this time, New Yorkers were all imported from Middle America. The concept of indigenous New York was a memory with character reruns playing out in New Jersey, or on the boondocks of the island by the children of the authentic or really good imposters. Fourth or fifth generation Greeks, Italians, Irish, Africans, and Eastern European Jews, with their accents and personalities, were extinct. They were replaced instead by kids who carried books on what it meant to be a New Yorker, watching episodes of a show from an ancient era, *Sex in the City*, on their life-units (portable devices that did everything), a show that detailed the rules of their coming adulthood. New York was their entitlement, so it seemed. They moved in droves and excluded the indigenous clans, their presence increased rents and sent the native tribes into ghetto fortresses known as 10k's, a legal term for low income housing (for residents longer than ten years) not officially revealed until 2030. With these new New Yorkers' innate suburban exclusion came an inability to perceive anyone else with the same human bond they shared amongst each other. Misili, an actual alien, seemed impervious to these people. Singing directly to them, she picked up on their condition.

I found myself locked
in your perceptions of my dreams...

She stood, her body covered, staring vacantly through an eye-hole fashioned through her head garb. What lay underneath remained a mystery until after the events that ensued. A sneering couple looked on, fresh out of the trendiest bar in the area, fashioned in a combination of styles throughout the latter twentieth century's subcultural movements, a mix of references from television and corporate music trends. They peered at Misili, who dressed unlike anyone. She was indeed the last of the originals.

"Is she a Muslim or what?" the female said to her attachment.

"Ugh! Just look at her. Couldn't she just wear a normal veil instead of that one-eyed one," replied the male counterpart.

"Yea, totally. Brownie Cyclops!!"

Where were her references? What band was she emulating? Who did she remind them of? Originality pissed off the posers.

Misili's brain stored a hyper-intelligence that was able to harness nearly 99.9% of the power of her mind. This ability came from the planet she originated from and allowed her to easily pick up conversations, thoughts, and emotions with ease. Misili was the Quadrophenic Antenna Girl.

The Veil!
The Veil!
The Veil!

She recited three times in a high-pitched voice then pressed a series of buttons on the modified Speak 'n Spell, tapping in a tempo. The distorted digital melody emanating from the device increased to punk rock speed. She began to turn in circles dramatically narrating in a low voice, "*On the day of souls, when the end comes to a close...*"

Her one visible eye peering back at the onlookers, *Narcissus will die leaving flesh to fry.*

Misili's turning became a whirl as her arms outstretched and she chanted:

Awful fools
Television has plucked your eyes
Whole damn life
Is commodified,
Are you sure I'm the one that you're looking at,
Are you sure I ain't from another planet!

The Veil, The Veil, The Veil
You can't get enough of this covered stuff!

The Veil, The Veil, The Veil

The late-night drunk post-college graduates and assorted "randoms" had never seen anything like this. As her whirl increased and her seemingly improvised lyrics echoed the train station, the middle-aged Ayanda Shiraz descended the stairs. The writer was returning home after another evening hobnobbing with the publishing elite, representing the fallen Muslim woman trying to remake herself in America. A position the publishers adored, sought out, and paid top dollar for.

"That was the night I first met the wretched little thing," Ms. Shiraz said to Jamil. Her voice shook from a tube feeding her through the esophagus.

Jamil was not the first to hear her confession. She had confessed countless times to the asylum chaplain who responded by telling her to say Hail Marys. When she explained that she had been the world's first acclaimed modern Muslim writer, the chaplain attempted to teach Shiraz the Hail Mary.

"If you want redemption, you must learn these prayers," he would insist. She would refuse, continuing instead to rant on and on about how she plotted the rise and fall of the "superhuman" Midhib and how Muslim women cannot recite Hail Marys for redemption.

"My veil…" Shiraz pronounced dramatically, "will be forced upon me again."

The chaplain, who would usually be empathetic during her confessions, encouraged her to say her own prayers, Muslim ones. They eluded her. She could not bring herself to remember any Muslim prayers so she scoffed at the chaplain, who would leave with an oppressive and ghastly impression of all things Muslim. First, Ayanda, world famous Arab writer, admits to murder then turns into a staunch feminist Islamo-Nazi, unable to even say a prayer. "So much for having a PhD," thought the chaplain walking out gripping his New Testament.

Jamil listened patiently as Shiraz continued the account of Misili, knowing the end would not be pleasant. He judged the old woman against his own contemporaries, a group labeled as the new sophisticated Muslim literati. This group would reinterpret Islamo-Futurism and make it their own, complete with Buster Al-Haq, the idyllic conceptual holographic artist who recreated the Afghanistan of 1975 into highly detailed tactile graphic 3D environments, or So'uad Tayiz, female poetess, who wrote of these recreated homelands in virtual space as if they were ancient ones with the same vitality and love of a Hafiz or a Rumi. Jamil, the blossoming journalist, and those around him, had not been born yet when Misili roamed the acid rain–soaked New York streets searching for memories, searching for rocks that resembled her planet, searching for home.

"That night, I offered her riches beyond her imagination. I told her she would be well taken care of and that my home could be her home," Ms. Shiraz said.

Jamil jotted some notes down and looked at the woman in the wheelchair, thinking of how this story would elevate him in his circle. "Is that the night you brought her under your wing, as you say?"

"No. The thing did not want glory. She refused my shelter and compassion that night, so I would sneak around and follow her, writing down the words that came out of her mouth."

"Why were you doing that?"

"I made her what she is! That girl's words were entering people's ears one way and coming out the other. Nobody paid her any mind with that little dark outfit and strange voice."

"Ms. Shiraz, I understand, but why were you writing down what she said?"

Ayanda glared at Jamil. The answer was simple, too simple.

"Young man, you are writing down what I say. Ask yourself, as writers, what do we need most?"

Ayanda was never a true writer—she was a hired gun and Misili was the perfect target. By stalking the alien poetess and copying down her manic episodes, Shiraz was able to write seven books on Islamic perception and female identification, and a trilogy on methods of the urban veil. All of these were written for Western presses intent on securing everything Islamic into a place of the tribalist past. Jamil would not discover her motivation until he reread Shiraz's books afterwards, but he responded to the immediate question of what writers need most.

"A story?" he answered.

Ayanda Shiraz continued, "The story of her fall begins and ends with me."

Misili Midhib hovered down Bowery and Houston, carrying a bag stuffed with assorted music-making and amplification devices. She whispered to herself, "Duality's premise is to subvert two opposing thoughts or ideas so as to create a distance between one and the other. The yin and the yang, the veiled woman and the sexually objectified woman."

Acid rain poured down on the carnival that is downtown on a Saturday night. Drunks bumped into Misili, foreigners in someone else's land taunted her at every turn. A man of Pakistani origin, a Muslim himself, yelled, "Damn *fundie!*"

She moved passed him unfazed, turning her covered head towards the man, her one-eye staring at him. The assimilated Pakistani froze as she sucked the life story out of him and played it back in milliseconds:

"He was born to an affluent Pakistani family who moved to Boston when they first came to the country. A businessman father stressed the importance of setting early career goals and his doctor mother pushed him towards the medical field."

Misili's eye shined, reflecting back the streetlights and passing taxicabs. Unlike a human eye, it lacked a lid.

The only thing that the Pakistani boy saw when looking into her hole was a white reflection of himself surrounding a black pupil that shined a psychic ray into his heart. He saw that his own overindulgent lifestyle was fermented by having everything and that his lack of identity was a result of too much insulation of his immigrant identity. He was more Pakistani than a Pakistani, an ABCD, American Born Chutney Desi, standing on a corner making fun of himself. His brown face glazed over pale as Misili continued on.

The trick, as she saw it, was to make eye contact only with those receptive to transformation or to shun them by turning the head covering to cover the eye. This way she kept the government from being involved and kept any actual physical contact from happening.

As she turned down 1st Avenue, frat boys in front of another bar yelled, "Take off that veil and let's fuck, you terrorist bitch!"

Misili decided to not turn this crew onto themselves. She ducked her head down and increased her advance, tapping the small bone that protruded from what could be a hip. The taps were in double-time to her steps, which were really perfect glides.

"Veiled girls are eroticized in this place," she whispered to herself as if communicating to an invisible counterpart. She tapped nine times like a double bass kick drum of a speedcore thrash drum track, almost machine-like. A green glow formed in between her touch and mystery body.

"They look at me because hiding one's form in public charges their voyeuristic libidinal drives. These types of minds cannot be quelled without thought rearrangement…"

The frat boys watched Misili hover away, only seeing her back.

"Dude, was she like floating or what?"

"Yeah, that was some weird shit, bro," the larger boy said to the smaller.

As she vanished into the darkness of buildings, the taps on her mystery body had a mesmerizing effect. Not that they were audible, but the space between the taps, the resonant interval that formed from the taps, echoed a silent vibration that performed a definite function, although imperceptible.

"Hot body, though," replied the smaller.

"What body? You saw a body?"

"Yea man, she was wearing a burq-ini!"

A passing cab lost control and pushed up full speed onto the sidewalk; the boys were in the direct path of the oncoming missile. Their screams were silenced by a sudden dumping of more rain and smashed glass.

The Brooklyn Exiles were to do a show for a corporate event at the Saint Regis Hotel, an uptown venue for the rich and affluent. They invited Misili to do her whirling act but mainly to reconnect on old times. A week earlier, the socialite magazine, *Scene*, published a picture of Misili performing her spoken-word at the Nuyorican Poets Cafe. The picture did not reproduce correctly. The shot was an orb of light on the stage, and written underneath was the caption "Some Muslim girl reading bullshit poetry (bad shot)." Readers of the magazine thought this phenomenon to be a hoax by the editor. They also did not like the word *Muslim* printed in their magazine. By this time, it was synonymous with all things alien and evil. Dov Tarney, the tight-pants, tight-shirt, all-cock editor put the word out to find Misili and get to the bottom of the phenomenon. "Was she indeed Muslim?" seemed to be more important than her inhuman reproduction in the photograph.

Jamil stretched out his neck as Shiraz narrated what seemed to be a story without end.

"I don't get this. So, was Misili becoming a celebrity? Where is this photograph? Did other publications track her?"

Shiraz responded, her voice in a permanent vibrato, "The Brooklyn Exiles event was a trap. Those trashy girls were the only way I could get Misili vulnerable enough to do what I wanted. They were the only people she spoke with freely."

"You used them to get to her?"

"We all used each other. They made off with a good amount of money."

"So you paid them, too?"

"Yes, but getting her to the venue was just the first part. I remember what happened next as if it were yesterday. The annual Asia Centric Association's

Publishers' ball, sponsored by the feminist organization, Operation Purple."

"They were responsible for giving out lingerie in Afghanistan during the war, right?" Jamil asked.

"Yes, an atrocious lot of misguided American women intent on 'saving' Muslim women. I always wondered why they wouldn't save themselves first, but the money was good."

"Money is always good, if used for good purposes," Jamil added.

Ayanda peered into Jamil's face, "No, young boy, money is always good."

The auditorium of the Saint Regis was packed with grey haired professors and intellectuals in framed glasses with one thing in common: none were Muslim yet most made careers off of books and documentaries on Muslims. On stage sat a panel of supposed Muslim scholars and experts, Ayanda Shiraz, Barbara Afiz, Robert Tenser, General Paul Thoratio, and a girl wearing a *hijab*, probably a nameless Afghan refugee, thrown in for authenticity. In front of them were fancy bottles of water and stylish microphones. The first speaker was Ayanda Shiraz herself.

"Honored guests, we would like to thank you for joining us this evening for a lively discussion on Islam and the West. I hope you have all read my latest book, *I Am Arab, I Am Sad*, and our guest lecturer Barbara Afiz's essay, *Attacks on Lesbians in Yemen*. Both are great reads and very informative on current events in the Islamic world."

Shiraz introduced the panel. "Barbara Afiz is the host of a nationally acclaimed radio show specializing on Muslim assimilation issues. She heads the National Arab Front and is married to Israeli bank baron Daniel Gideon." Barbara leaned into her mic, "Thank you Ayanda, I would just like to correct you—I not only head the Arab Front but I also started it. Thank you for having me."

The dark figure of Misili entered the hall. She was not hovering but rather slowly stepped into a dark corner and sat on the floor, placing her heavy bag of devices beside herself. Ayanda glanced at her, then back to her presenters.

"Robert Tenser is a *New York Times* bestselling author. His books, *Worshipping Black Rocks: The World's Most Intolerant Religion*, and *Muhammad, EXPOSED!* take brave looks at the reasons why Islam and the West are at odds."

Robert leaned into his mic and with a Texan accent said, "Thank you Ayanda, always a pleasure. Might I add, I loved your last book *I Am Arab, I Am Sad.* You are also brave for telling the truth of living in your type of race."

People in the audience clapped. Misili tapped nine times, activating the resonant interval.

Those that noticed Misli became uncomfortable and could not get themselves to move, let alone clap. Security for the event began communicating over their wireless devices. "Suspicious person in the auditorium."

Misili was at first covered by the darkness of the unlit corner and her garb. Never a girl to be confused, she began channeling the thoughts and emotions of the crowd around her. Upon hearing the security guards' communication, she sent psychic interference on that frequency so as to prevent violence against her.

The Afghan refugee girl approached the microphone and began to tell a story of being tortured by the Taliban and saved by U.S. Marines.

"I remember how bad it was before the Americans came. I was kidnapped by seven bearded men, who said they were Taliban and that my veil was on too tight..."

Misili stared at the girl with her one eye, seeing through her like an X-ray, bones and blood and a rapidly beating heart, indicating one of two things: she was nervous, or she was lying. The mystical poetess then tuned into the supposed refugee's thought pattern. Flashes of the girl's moments before the event began to hit her like a film. A dark figure handed the girl a check for an undisclosed amount of money. The girl took the check and was told to make the story sad. Misili hears, "And try to cry for the photographers. It would help appeal to their human side."

Misili went deeper, into the heart of the story. The girl is indeed an Afghan refugee (that much was true) but no memories existed to back up her claims of kidnapping and oppression. She left Afghanistan by her own will, on a first class ticket out of Kabul, with a group of Western feminists wearing Operation Purple shirts. Misili dredged through the girl's memories, looking for the story she was telling the mesmerized audience.

Meanwhile, the supposed refugee wept onstage, unable to continue the story once she started to describe a rape scene. Ayanda Shiraz comforted her, cradling the girl's head, and says into the microphone, "As you can see, the hard hand of Islamic fascism can be traumatic to these young girls."

The crowd nodded in approval, some professors joining with the girl in crying at the hell that is this imagined Afghanistan. Someone yelled, "Islamic perverts!"

Ayanda responded, "Now, now, there is some good in Islam. Let's hear from General Paul Thoratio on our progress in colonizing Turkey for acceptance on the global economy. Paul."

A highly decorated general stepped to the mic. Paul Thoratio, born to a military intelligence family responsible for the splitting of Ottoman lands after the empire fell. "Distinguished guests, Turkey has been in the grips of an unhealthy secularism since the radical revolution of Kemal Ataturk in the early part of last century. By shedding their Arabic roots and removing Sharia Law from their courts, I propose, they have actually taken a step back. Turkey needs an American president *and* needs to give Constantinople back to the West. These are the only solutions for their entrance in wonderful pluralistic Western civilization. It will also be cool to visit that big mosque." He coughed and drank water out of the fancy bottle.

Misili's thought breach stopped prematurely as Ayanda appeared in her view. She recognized the Arab writer but could not access her thoughts. Misili mumbled to herself, "The woman from the train station."

Jamil wrote on his notepad, "Research time and date of Operation Purple meeting in 2018. Shiraz's claims need to be fact-checked. Are there recordings of the security cameras or communications from that night?"

"Why are you writing so much? I have not yet finished," Shiraz curiously asked.

"Nothing, just some notes. You said Misili showed up for a sideshow thing. Based on what you said, wouldn't she leave when the Brooklyn Exiles were not present to greet her?"

"Nonsense. I had the thing in my mental grip the second she walked into the room."

Jamil's eyes widened. How could Shiraz have prevented psychic access by this alien intelligence? Somewhere in her testimony later, he would find the answer.

As the event drew to a close Misili stood up, unraveled by the rhetoric of the panel, and yelled, "Ban the Academics! They speak of lies told on the shoulders of dead children! The general is a reptile hiding underneath human skin! The radio host is a self-hating opportunist! That girl is not a refugee! She was brought here to lie to all of you!"

Six security guards approached Misili from all sides of the auditorium as the alien girl made her pronouncement to the crowd of shocked intelligentsia. Misili tapped in stride with the pace of the security men's steps and they mysteriously stopped.

"Who is that strange hooded girl?" asked Barbara to Ayanda. Shiraz smiled and said, "Watch."

Misili continued, "You cannot justify your war on an ideology by creating a fantasy enemy, by paying for your scripted fantasies!"

Shiraz basked in the pure rage emanating from Misili, waiting for a gem of knowledge to come out to which she could dedicate her next book.

Misili began to turn in circles, now the center of attention, and recited:

A new world is promised
without the scourge of the insane
but an old world is surfaced
when the insane are drained
of their right to dream
by the sellers of fantasy
con men dressed up
in the veil of democracy.

Shiraz jumped to the microphone and called off security. "People!" she yelled, "Get a hold of yourselves, and let's hear this girl out!"

Misili's casual turning quickened to a whirl as her form became nearly incomprehensible. A whirl of wind spinning in circles, floating inches off the ground, singing what seemed to be a prayer in a foreign tongue:

Al haq zeni tekmet sizen Allah'in,
Ayla hoon janim tekmekdet 'dan bagla'dim.

Ringing of a foreign Turkish tongue, none of her words made sense to the onlookers who were entranced by the physics of what she was singing.

"*La illa ḥa illalah!*" she repeated louder and louder and louder while rising even further.

* * *

Jamil could not make sense of the story. He seemed dazed.

"You're telling me she's floating in the middle of the room basically doing a sufi dzikr?"

"If you stop interrupting me, I can finish the story, young Muslim," demanded the wrinkled Shiraz. "The thing was a master of the resonant interval."

"Hold on. That's an Islamic prayer, the *ilahi*, that she's saying."

"Yes, it is, but she was not Muslim—at least as we know it today."

"So she was speaking in some alien Arabic variant and then went into the traditional chant?"

"She was speaking in the tongue of her native planet and exhibiting what I was later taught by her. It was a method of mass cleansing, energy purification via linear tactility. Now, may I finish?"

Jamil was aggravated. His notes turned into scribbles, his scribbles to chicken scratch on a page of word associations all too complex to make a story out of. His brows furrowed as the female face appeared on the electronic walls, "Sorry to interrupt, five minutes left for visiting hours. Thank you." The face dissolved into a scrolling text of financial details and images of war.

"Just tell me how you killed her, Shiraz! I don't need these delusional fantasies from the mind of a managed schizophrenic!"

Ayanda leaned back in her wheelchair gasping for air. She placed an air mask on her face and inhaled deeply, tapping on her hip as the machine sent oxygen into her lungs.

"You anger me, Jamil. I do not deserve to be yelled at. I am an old woman."

"I apologize. Just tell me how you killed her and I'll be leaving. We only have a couple of minutes left and I believe you are wasting my time."

"This interview is over, young Muslim. I hope some big publisher recognizes you after you write this story that I just gave you. Now, goodbye."

Shiraz flipped a switch on her wheelchair and defiantly turned around, rolling off towards a wall on the other side of the room. She ordered the computer, "Open window viewport. Location, Japanese gardens." The wall transformed into a window overlooking a Japanese garden, complete with waterfalls and rock gardens.

Jamil packed his notepad away and placed his pen in his shirt pocket, lifting himself off the chair.

"You know, Ms. Shiraz, the world would like to know what happened to Misili Midhib."

Ayanda Shiraz, the writer who once was the messenger of the essence of an alien girl named Misili Midhib, perhaps a time-traveler whose portal had a glitch, perhaps just an unborn being transported to our time by a global silent need.

The self-confessed murderer of the alien poetess rested her eyes on the world outside her viewport window, watching digital doves fly past a holographic reality on the walls of a crazy ward. The doves chased one another with a preprogrammed playfulness, tapping each other's feathers as they moved. An error in the coding made one blue instead of white. The blue one chased a white one, pecked at it to get attention, then dove down as the white one followed.

Ayanda laughed, ignoring Jamil's question. "There are no blue doves, young Muslim."

The journalist walked towards the door. "Thank you for your time, Ms. Shiraz." As he exited, the chaplain waiting on the other side of the door quickly looked at Shiraz, then at Jamil, who nodded negatively. The door was shut.

Shiraz stared at the projection of an imagined reality, closing one eye and opening the other wider, laughing at her own reflection. "Only almonds dressed as birds take flight when timing meets faith."

Jamil walked down the hall convinced that Ayanda Shiraz had fabricated the once legendary Misli. His eyelids closed for a brief second. "No eyelids? She said Misli had no eyelids!"

A whisk of air brushed across Jamil's face followed by the humming of an atonal voice.

Narcissus will die ...

He opened his eyes, catching the last shadow of a certain something, or somebody, vanishing into the ether.

TOM SMALL, MICRO-CRUSADER

When the FedEx truck pulled up to the Small family's plush Connecticut home, Tom, an only man-child, was giving libations in his makeshift shrine. The shrine's authenticity was questionable, having no particular religious affiliation and located inside a shrub on his lawn. Tom hunched into the shrubs and placed a horribly halved coconut shell filled with water at the center, where a badly framed photo of Sir Lawrence of Arabia stood.

"It's tough being white," Tom said as he touched Sir Lawrence, remembering a time when liberating Arabs was just a matter of finding the right cockney charm. He delicately pulled the frame out and replaced the picture with a ripped photograph. A chipmunk skull lay nearby, remnants from Tom's Santeria phase. Currently in his "white guilt" phase, Mr. Small's offerings became less morbid. No longer seeking bloody revenge on his fencing team comrades, he rotated framed pictures of fallen Cherokee warriors, assassinated Latin American revolutionaries, and a host of infamous British colonialists, bringing them all water in coconut shells (as if the act of gracious offerings would somehow relieve him of his guilt).

"It's tougher being brown, my Talibani brother," he says, dabbing his finger into the shell and touching it to the picture for the day: a detainee who committed suicide by hanging himself at the Guantanomo Bay detention facility.

His interruptions were numerous. Mama Small, fresh from her tour of the Connecticut hillside (a parking lot with two bagel shops and a yeast mill) sang karaoke to the *Sound of Music* soundtrack, yodeling off-pitch in the background to "The Lonely Goatherd" song, "*One little girl in a pale pink coat heard, Lay ee odl lay ee odl lay hee hoo!*" This continued as the FedEx man stood over the shrub, examining the corduroy shoes that stuck out from it.

"Tom Small?" asked the deliveryman.

"I need to be put under surveillance," a voice inside the shrub shrine said.

"Pardon?"

"Who do I call? Is Rummy still around?"

"Sir? Are you all right? I have a package for a Tom Small. Are you him?"

Tom rustled himself backwards out of the shrine with a grace akin to that of a do-do landing.

"Need help there, buddy?"

Tom leapt horizontal against the deliveryman, grabbed the pen and signed off.

"Were you sent by the company? I have a plan. Tell them I have a plan!"

Puzzled, the man handed over the package, reviewing the signature. Tom grabbed it and ran inside the mansion, echoes of his mother wailing, *…soon her Mama with a gleaming gloat heard, Lay ee odl lay ee odl lay hee hoo!*

Tom ran up the gold-gilded staircase, through the highly decorated hallways, and into the "family karaoke room" where Mama Small fiddled with the CD player, restarting the song. Tom stormed in, throwing the box at his hapless mother and standing defiantly as it bounced off the floor.

"I'm sick and tired of this mundane freedom and access to all kinds of resources!"

The song began again. His mom, a frail woman of privilege, wearing a muumuu and yellow galoshes, turned toward him. "Tom, talk to your father. Can't you see I'm with Mother Mary?"

Tom fell on his knees, going from point A to Z in one second. "Please… I hate you… Someone… take away my resources and render me helplessly dependent on a system of external control!"

High on a hill was a lonely goatherd, Lay ee odl lay ee odl lay hee hoo!

"Aaaaaaaaaaa!!!!!!" yelled Tom over his mother's song as he ran down the hall in frustration.

"Little Tommy," Momma thought, "worshipping invisible friends in bushes and making wild demands."

Tom arranged for a private jet to take him to Daddy Small's office. He sat in his father's big leather chair high atop Halaliburton, a multinational oil contracting company, in their Texas headquarters. He wore an orange jumpsuit and a leopard skin headband.

"Eye of the tiger, dad!"

Both papa and son growled at each other, making tiger claws jestingly.

"So you want to go to Guantanamo?"

Tom shrugged. "Don't say it like that, like I'm voluntarily going. I'm a thought terrorist. Zwahiri and me are best buds. I can run circles around you, Dad!"

Papa Small, confused yet preprogrammed to always look like the illustration of himself hanging across his desk—a photoshopped picture of Biggie Smalls hugging him—considered it, squeezing a koosh ball.

"You got it Tom-o, but don't say I didn't warn you."

Tom pulled out an Arabic-English dictionary and flipped through the pages.

"Last time you went to Gitmo, things didn't work out so well. I just want you to remember that."

Tom found the word he was searching for. "*Shook ran.* That means thank you, Dad, now get Rummy on the phone."

Within three hours, Papa Small had arranged a private jet to drop ship his son into the Gitmo base. The soldiers had been prepped on Lil' Tom's needs and living conditions from a previous stint at the facility.

Apparently, Tom, under the impression that he was a modern-day Lawrence of Arabia mixed with the heroic children's movie *The Karate Kid* (the original) forced female soldiers to sexually humiliate him. "Like the pictures from Abu Ghraib," he insisted.

Staff Sergeant Linda Calhoun stood over Tom, who was reclined over backwards wearing a blindfold.

"I don't know if this legal, Tom," she said, holding a taser pointed at Tom's ass.

Tom, unable to see, turned toward Linda. "You need to torture me, humiliate me, just like you did in Iraq. My people will not be humiliated without me."

Linda looked through the two-way mirror Tom's dad had set up in his cell and saw two flashes, which indicated that she go ahead with whatever

Tom wanted.

This bizarre Abu Ghraib re-enactment got everybody in a bit of trouble after Tom anonymously sent photos to a French newspaper.

Under the recent instructions of Papa Small, all Gitmo staff were to act as if Tom was an inmate, at least in front of him. Any demands he made, no matter how preposterous, were to be acted upon immediately. He arrived handcuffed and chained, by his own volition, his leopard skin headband on, frowning.

Staff Sergeant Linda Calhoun greeted him.

"Welcome back, Tom, didn't get enough last time?"

Tom raised his gaze, giving her his best tortured-victim glare. "I am Abu Fat-Toosh, not this Tom character you speak of."

"So, you're Abu today, Tom? And what do you want us to do this time?" she asked. Tom looked at the Cuban sky for answers, twiddling his nose from the dust of the helicopter taking off next to him.

"I'd like to be put in solitary…" Linda jotted notes as he continued, "but I will protest and demand a lawyer."

"Okay, and when you make this demand should we actually get you a lawyer?"

"No, no. Shut up. Then I will go on a food fast to protest being in solitary and not having proper representation."

"Ok, food fast. Do you have any special orders for your fast?"

"Cream cheese? Can you do that?"

"Sure," Linda notes.

"I'll need to be force-fed the cream cheese, though, just like you're doing to the detainees," he adds.

"Well, not exactly Tom, but whatever you say."

"Then, finally, I would like a forced confession behind closed doors by a staff of Pentagon intel."

The Staff Sergeant, now Tom's torture nanny, nodded affirmatively. "Do you have any details on how we should force the confession?"

Tom returned his gaze to the tortured victim angle. "I will confess to it all: the poverty, the pain, the suffering. I, Abu Fat-Toosh single-handedly sunk the Titanic, Atlantic, and Siegfried and Roy."

"Will that be all, Tom?"

"I also need new clothes. This orange outfit no longer suits me. Get me a red *shalwar kameze* and a unicycle. I like to keep fit but also look fabulous. I'm ready for my cage-up, Ms. Calhoun."

The man-child, Tom Small, was gently placed into a specially made "solitary" cell complete with high speed internet and a bagel vending machine that would occasionally blurt out of its internal speakers, "You want cream cheese on that, buddy?" and eject a slow glob of rotten cream cheese onto the floor.

Tom sat across from the glob, staring vacuously at the slow drips falling from the squirt tube.

Bastard Americans. They are trying to break my will with the bagel machine. I know it, but it won't work.

Tom leapt into the air screaming, "ISLAMO-FUTURIST HADITH NUMBER THREE HUNDRED EIGHTY NINE: And they will try to break your will with a faulty bagel vending machine but ALAS be steadfast for God will provide miles of pure and fresh cream cheese in PARADISE!"

The door to the cell opened, and three figures in biochemical protective suits rushed Tom, pushing him under the cheese spouts.

"You're gonna eat, and you're gonna like it!" said one of the guards, pushing him down.

"GET YOUR INFIDEL PAWS OFF ME!" the man-child yelled, as written in the "Abu Fat Toosh & Cream Cheese" script he had faxed them a few hours earlier.

Another guard takes Tom's head, as directed on page four, and stuffed it under the spout.

"Open up, Tommy boy!"

"No! No!" Tom cried melodramatically, his acting skills running a bit off the charts.

"Squeezy sleazy!" replied the third guard pushing the cream cheese eject button, Tom getting coated with the cheese.

"Jewish cream cheese conspiracy!" he managed to yell before being silenced by a mountain of the rich breakfast accessory substance.

Jewish... cre—am, ch—eese, con—sp...

Guard Two, forgetting his final lines of dialogue, slickly took out a copy of the script and read aloud in an untrained actor monotone, "Where's your Allah now?"

During this, his second stay at the makeshift prison facility, Tom managed to befriend one of the men held without justification or official charges set against him. Most of the Gitmo inmates still had no idea why they were being held. Over 800 in total, they were restricted from any media or from communicating with their aunties, flamenco partners, or lawyers. Tom made it a point to speak to a certain inmate during the allowed afternoon prayers.

"What are you in for?" Tom asked, now wearing a ridiculous red *shalwar kameze* decorated with paisley Persian truffles and lace inlets. He stood alongside the praying man. The man, with a full beard and a *kufi*, turned his head silently, whispering the initial *ilahi*.

Tom, not getting an answer back, imitated the man's motions, also whispering to himself but in the gibberish only he understood.

As the inmate leaned down prostrate, Tom did the same thing.

As the man sat on his knees giving his final *rakat*, Tom did the same. Lastly, as the man palmed his face, finishing his prayer off, Tom did the same, except exhaling loudly with a sigh, trying to get the man's attention.

"Wooo-weeee! Now that's what I call a prayer." Tom slammed the man's shoulder in an over-compensatory fraternal nudge of approval. "Good stuff, huh? Wanna trade Taliban war stories?"

Tom rolled on his unicycle, keeping balance while staying fabulous in front of the inmate, who was forced to accompany Tom. "Took a good amount of time to learn this move..." Tom says, flipping the unicycle with a jump. The man never said a word. Tom shrugged off the lack of responsiveness and resolved to a one-sided chat at the electric barbed wire picnic chair lounge area. Tom went on and on about made up stories of fighting off Russian occupiers in Chechnya.

"Bastard commies, they didn't know what was coming." Tom explained at a table, pulling out G.I Joes from his lace-inlaid pockets. He moved one gnarly looking action figure (Zartan the swamp mercenary) onto the top barbwire. "We were in the trees—like ghosts—and when enough of the commies were under us, we attacked!" He threw the toy on the dusty ground.

Guards watched the inmate and Tom, making sure the inmate endured Tom's tirade. "The Russians were running off scared but our team of Chechen rebels had secret powers, granted to us by the Viking overlords of Spain…"

As the made-up stories continued, Tom lost all regard for time and place of the actual facts he was discussing. The inmate would periodically fall asleep, and guards would tase him back to consciousness. Tom went on unfazed— and untased.

"Zarqawi and me, boy, were those the days! You had to be there. Hold on, were you?" The random Afghan detainee looked at Tom, no response.

"I'm glad you're so open. You know, less than thirty percent of Americans even know a Muslim. Crazy, right?"

The guards tased the man back from his sixtieth attempt to nap. As the detainee popped back up, a shadow loomed over all of them. Tom looked to the Cuban skies. It was a United States humanitarian aid plane.

The guard started to panic, a voice over the loudspeaker system, "Broken Arrow! BROKEN ARROW!"

The guards looked at Tom and the inmate, then at each other.

"FOXTROT!" said Guard One.

"ALPHA!" yelled Guard Two.

"ZEBRA!" screamed Guard Three.

"CREAM CHEESE!" replied the detainee, coming to wakefulness for a moment, then nodding back off to sleep.

The plane puttered along as the weight of its cargo burst at its seams. Tons of pure Philadelphia cream cheese, meant for starving kids in Brazilian favelas, tumbled out in waves.

One massive wave of cream cheese descended on Tom and the detainee who had fallen asleep—for what might've been his final nap.

"CREAM CHEESE ATTACK!" Tom yelled, doing karate moves, trying to defend himself from the aerial bombardment. He tried to mount his unicycle to escape, but to no avail. The cream cheese wave squelched them all!

The guards abandoned both men. Gitmo was covered in the largest schmeer of cream cheese. So much that Tom was up to his neck in it. The detainee and the rest of Guantanamo were all gone, trapped under mountains of white gooey breakfast substance. Tom turned his head in time to witness the plane swooshing head first into a hill of its own cheese. All was quiet on the Cuban shores. Tom tried to wiggle out but it was futile—the cream cheese was thick and overpowering.

Poor Tom Small, a victim of his own deep need to experience the pain of our current enemies, found himself cemented in a congealing combination of dairy and scallions.

The horror. The horror.

ISA, AMERICAN TURK

1. Drifts

"In the colonial world, the emotional sensitivity of the native is kept on the surface of his skin like an open sore which flinches from the caustic agent; and the psyche shrinks back, obliterates itself and finds outlet in muscular demonstrations which have caused certain very wise men to say that the native is a hysterical type."

– Frantz Fanon, "Concerning Violence"
The Wretched of the Earth (1963)

I examine myself in the mirror clenching my teeth together and smiling wide to get a view of that damn tooth; I look insane. The orthodontist calls it a *mesial drift*. Only Central Asian skull morphologies are susceptible to it, so he claims before handing me a quote for ten grand to fix it partially. The complete solution, he says, is to wear permanent metal retainers for the rest of my life. Then and only then, can I assure complete facial conformity. The quote was written on an invoice with a glossy logo of a picture of Jerry Seinfeld smiling back at me.

"Tooth Zone 3000, Because Image Control is central to self-control."

Now Jerry's fish eye face spreads my mouth open every night as he repeats their motto, *Image Control is central to self-control, Image Control is central to self-control.* I panic and run to the bathroom, where all my teeth begin falling out to the sound of my own screams. In the mirror—the back of my head. More teeth fall out. In the mirror—the back of my head again.

Damn art history books got Magritte all up in my subconscious.

I wake up at three a.m. like clockwork and check out the protruder. The tooth appears further and further away from its rightful place each time I look.

Has the drift started yet?

Perhaps it's run amok.

I don't have ten grand!

The rush of who I am attacks me in waves. My skull, my teeth, my eyes… not like the kids I grew up with… Thought explosions… Neural storms like photographs of alienated strangers blowing up in your head all at once. I've moved eight times since 9/11. I technically belong to multiple ethnic groups.

I may be impotent.

I don't know that for a fact but saying *I was an impudent young man* would be paying too much homage to Dostoyevsky. Paying homage to foreigners may make me look too exotic. Also, those damn Russians killed my people off—or so around 2,500 desperate *diasporic-addicts* and myself would like to believe.

My overuse of cell phone technology has resulted in the lowering of my brain cells and sperm count. I am dwindling away, cracking apart, and losing my mind.

None of it is my fault, I think as I try to push the tooth back into place again.

It's the two gigahertz low level alpha brain wave interrupting technology of the iPhone that bake my thoughts with radiation. It's the childhood conditioning to live for lust, pursuit, and the illusion of fleshy happiness. It's the mark of the ethnic. It's 9/11 and George Bush and his wife. It's my dad and all his wives. It's my mother and all her husbands. It's my ancestors rotting in Russian train cars. It's all the loss piled a mile high like carcasses of dead cheetahs living in multiple dimensions of half-assed universes. The only thread that connects me together are the photographs of alienated strangers blowing up in my head all at once. I'm living in a protected little abstract shell, a New York nomad, happily discontent with the system dreaming away.

My shell happens to fit into what the current version of Oxford dictionary's first partial and second definition for the term *ethnic* is:

eth·nic

1c. Of, relating to, or distinctive of members of such a group: *ethnic* restaurants; *ethnic* art.

Now number two strikes me as the alarming one for its bold admittance of the way of the world.

2. Relating to a people not Christian or Jewish; **heathen**.

Now, not only should I own a restaurant one day and say things like, "Would you like more pita?" I discover I am also a heathen. In the Stan Lee Marvel Universe worldview, a heathen is what Spider-Man fights against, the villains of a childish mythology. Stick a stake in my heart and roast me for dinner, I'm done.

* * *

Brooklyn, New York, September 11th, 1981, I was four. My father had to break into his own apartment, where my mom and her new boyfriend were just beginning to throw a live lobster into a boiling cauldron. Up until that point, my short life had been filled with episodes of my parents battling each other on a near daily basis. When Dad finally left, Mom didn't waste time finding the next guy. Mom, the new guy, and I spent that day visiting the Twin Towers, and I remember looking over the city from the deck scared shitless; a strong wind would come and blow me onto the spiked trenches past the security gate. I held my mom's hand the whole time, sneering at the guy thinking, *Look at this new degenerate role model.* I'm supposed to be happy. I'm supposed to bite the bullet and just bond. Society beware! If you have a kid, expect to keep your shit together for the first five years of the kid's life, at least. Two weeks after the separation, here we are overlooking New York and this son-of-a-bitch is pretending to be my father.

She bought me a tiny shirt with a glittery print of the towers. The words *I Love New York* splashed across the glittered image of the buildings.

I swear the red crustacean was screaming as dad kicked in the door and came stomping down the hallway into the kitchen. Dad had not been around since the separation. I guess he was getting ready for inflicting pain. This other guy, taller than my real dad, was weak in his soul, a nameless shadow man that never really existed.

I remember my father, a young Mediterranean Carlos Santana type during the Woodstock years, ran into the room and grabbed the guy by his throat, smashing his lanky head into a glass frame.

"Fucking asshole!" Dad yelled, The picture inside the frame was of grandpa, who now became a sponge for shadow man's bloody cranium. As I watch glass break into the air, the other man's skull being thrust into it, shards and blood flying in slow motion, I freeze time. My cornea takes in moments, pupils dilating into focus on the blood. New synapses form in my brain. Neural nets form connections to associative mechanisms that flashed like electric bursts birthing the beginnings of relationship addiction, violence, identity confusion, and insecurity.

Mom wrestled with my blood-soaked father, previously her poet, her lover, her husband, now replaced by a bloody shadow in her own soundtrack of lobster's screams. The stepdad lay concussing on the ground in a pool of his own blood, staining grandfather's face in the photo.

Ironic.

What's become of us, as if God was commenting through my young eyes. *Is this the better life they wanted for themselves? Who is at fault, and when will it end? When will my life begin?*

Right now.

Before I know it, I'm kidnapped and thrown into a '76 red Mustang filled with first generation Turkish men dressed like disco hippies telling me everything would be alright.

"You're safe now!" says Birol, leaning me into the backseat.

"Upside Down" by Miss Diana Ross was in mid-chorus on the radio. Dad was outside the car still yelling his latest great points to my mom who was dealing with shards of glass lodged in her new man's skull, a stolen son, and a broken home. Everyone was guilty, and I yearned for that calm family walking down the street.

Birol's mustache bounced over his lips as the odor of rampantly applied cologne filled the air. Great. I was beneath the umbrella now, and it said *Odiferous Mustache People Under Here.*

This was dad's best friend, both from the same town in Turkey. Both learned English, played in an awful rock band, and womanized using the best of their ethnic novelties. Birol's sister had an affair with my dad, one of the reasons for all the pain of my first years.

Usually, when I set off to analyze Turks, I separate myself from them because of this great terrible episode that befell me. Today I've disowned all of them, written them off as foreign trailer trash that couldn't control their dicks and pussies, whores and monsters, symbols of all that is wrong and worth unlearning. No child wants to be the subject of a violent domestic coup d'état.

I think about the moment my dad asked me where I got the shirt with the glittery thick print of the towers.

"Mommy got it for me," I say. It was the first time he noticed something I was wearing.

"Nice shirt," comments Birol.

"Mommy got you that shirt?" my dad asks again as if to imply that the son-of-a-bitch might have.

I forget the question. Four years old, never yelled at by my dad, I've literally been alive for around thirty-five thousand hours. That's like watching *Indiana Jones and the Temple of Doom* eleven thousand times. *My front tooth feels loose,* I think, *the tooth fairy will come and save me.* My attention span takes over—something with the shirt. I look down at my chest, the glittery shape of *I Love New York* sprawled across. Dad looks over at Birol.

"That fucker gave him that shirt," Dad says.

"Let's just get to Long Island and—" Birol remarks before being thrust ahead as the car skids, my father leaning his arm back and ripping the shirt from my chest, the momentum smashing my face against the back seat. The tooth snaps off into my throat as my dad tosses the shirt out of the window.

"My son is not a goddamn tourist!" he yells, looking back at me briefly.

I get myself back up on the seat and watched the shirt fly away, getting further and further away as we drive onto the Long Island Expressway. The tooth gets coughed up and I cup it in my hands to place under whatever pillow I end up sleeping on that night.

"Isa, that was an ugly shirt. Daddy will buy you real clothes, not like that one." My father's tone is soft now as if everything is back in balance.

Birol looks at me, smiles, and hands me a painter's shirt he pulls from a bag. "Here, wear this. You're your own man, Isa," he says.

Not even a boy yet, and suddenly these fools are trying to tell me I'm a man. *Will I have to start paying rent now?*

Considering that I was *no tourist* I should have felt justified and entitled to any geography. As this memory etched itself into my frontal lobes, I should have been destined to never feel like a tourist anywhere, particularly at those times in my life trapped in a family member's backseat, half naked and staring out a window. I should have learned what the adults were pushing into me, but I didn't. Their childish needs and conflicts overrode whatever lessons they had for me.

This is all I learned: *Manhood equals busted teeth and beatdowns.* I was a tourist, worse even, a stranger in a strange land with even stranger people around me.

*   *   *

Seventeen years later, I'm a college slacker gasping for air in the passenger seat of Ron *"The man"* Torter, who just purchased a Buick Regal for $50 with a broken catalytic converter (which was the main reason for it being so cheap). That father I just told you about, he's been imprisoned for years now; he's as much a shadow as the other son-of-a-bitch, who died of a crack overdose when I was nine. I'm living with my mom, and we communicate by fighting relentlessly, so I stay clear of my home to stay clear of the fists and hot irons. Tonight, I'm twenty-one. Tonight, carbon monoxide fills the car's interior as we make our way down the Belt Parkway in Brooklyn. Throbbing Gristle plays back industrial noise music on a broken cassette deck hanging from wires.

"Gonna puke!" I gasp. Ron, my only ever bald Mormon friend, laughs, and his piercing, Kalamazoo-born blue eyes provide a temporary equanimity.

"It's not that bad," he replies.

I dry heave as the Verrazano Bridge passes by. Leon in the backseat displaying none of the ill symptoms I was having, probably due to how high he was.

"Bro, you need to calm down. It's all in your head," Leon says.

"No, I think it's the noxious fucking fumes emitting from the hood of this piece of shit," I squawk.

"See, that's the genetic difference between us, Isa," Leon retorted. "I'm gonna make a mark in the world. Guys like you are just going to panic at every turn."

"What's that got to do… with…" I said, sucking my words into the dry heave. "Pull over!" I yelled. This was it.

My dad echoes in my head, *My son is not a damn tourist!* I was not nearly as ethnic as Leon Muskind accused me of being. Muskind was a career student, after all—thirty years old, still living in his mother's basement in Bensonhurst, and much resembling a stumpy hobbit. I compared him in my mind to an early paramecium type man with an affliction for role-playing games and Tolkien.

Dan screeched to a stop, turns to me compassionately, "You gonna puke?" I threw the door open and thought about pulling Leon out of the backseat and crushing his head with my steel-toe boots. Alas, the nausea took over such that I would hurl, dry heave, and then hurl again.

"Ha, ha! Immigrant!" Leon commented from behind me. I turned my head, wiping drips of vomit off my lips. Leon's image flickered as I looked at him again, as if he was being broadcast and the signal had temporary interference, a reality glitch. Buzzzzzzz! I spit the remaining bits of undigested food out. The feeling of this reality being a controlled sitcom subsided with the puke smell.

I was too green in the face that night to put up much resistance to being called a wetback. Leon did eventually catch some of my knuckles, but that didn't happen quickly. I'd admit that much. The use of my fists as a solution to fixing the world's accusations was not my natural inclination. It was sort of uncontrolled hysteria built up over years, or so I came to believe, as did my re-flexes. My attacks were without hesitation, and despite being a trained fighter, I would aim my blows at the accuser's most vulnerable areas. Every time I felt alienated because of my face or place in the pecking order, I grew more lethal. I've broken bottles on heads, used aluminum baseball bats too. I've knocked enormous guys to the ground with pipes, knees, elbows, and whatever hurt the other guy most. For a while it was a game, a sociopathic game, but with Leon, it was the principle. The outdated concept he had that I was some kind of immigrant. Although it was well known I was born in the United States. At one time, his people were first-generation and my knuckles felt he should re-member this. Several months after I puked carbon monoxide–spiked bile, my little college circle of misanthropes and overly-educated sycophants would gather in Marine Park, Brooklyn for all night revelries—drum circles with kids that couldn't bang out a beat if they tried and ex-yeshiva Jewish girls ex-periencing how the Goyam get down. There we were, the South Brooklyn Breakfast Club in mindless mindfulness. Each second a huge phony epiphany playing some early nineties soundtrack in our minds. We had vested interests and similar hang-ups. Our parents were all retarded regardless of who was wealthier, and despite our class status, we substituted family for each other. I don't recall what I said or did, but Leon called me a foreigner again.

The drums stopped.

"Isa, what's the matter?" asked a friend as my synapses began their storms. My eyes locked, fixed towards Leon as the scene around him dimmed to only the oppressor in a sea of black.

"Isa, calm down dude," said another faceless voice from within the abyss. "He's just joking around!" I didn't hear anything though.

A moment of silence, then I threw my body at poor Leon, bursting with deadly force. My blows carried him upwards and back, smashing to the ground. Over his head the bottoms of my combat boots shot down, cracking his nose cartilage. I felt a touch on my shoulder, perhaps someone trying to call it off but it didn't matter. I fired with impossible accuracy into the un-protected area just below the man's breastbone. Had I continued, the verac-ity of my attacks would have torn lungs, crushed arteries, and possibly burst his heart.

I was dragged away in a near hallucinatory state. My college days ending in that park that night.

Isa became a reactionary. The music was over. My trauma created trauma to others, to some my exhibition that night was the craziest thing they had ever seen. Over the course of my life, events like this have made permanent impressions on those that have known me; so much so that in order to survive, I must constantly seek new beginnings that I inevitably crush from these impulses.

Leon eventually committed suicide with his girlfriend several years later. They supposedly fucked in a public park then both jumped off an elevated train track onto an oncoming train, reciting Bilbo Baggins exit speech to his hobbit friends in *The Hobbit*. In a morbidly romantic way, Leon and the girl's remains lay gnarled and sprawled out across McDonald Avenue. He made his mark, albeit rendered useless and pathetic after the streets were cleaned of halved livers and blended bone and muscle fragments.

Comments intended to make me feel or seem foreign in any way have since been met with ultra-violence that comes in the form of unexpected quick response attack spasms.

*   *   *

Tonight, I continue to examine my mesial drift in the mirror, just like I've done every night since reality thinned out and the *broadcasts* increased. My rear bicuspid is cracked from a particularly bad beatdown. I wish I could smash out four teeth and push the rest into place. Fucked up teeth hurt. The pain stops being pain and just becomes a state of mind, an unfinished, incomplete and chaotic state of mind. Violence may be learned phenomenon, but tonight I want to break shit because of my face, because I am simply not like the rest of America. The pain I've inflicted on people since childhood, all the way to Leon and beyond, may be due to that first memory photograph of dad slamming that son-of-a-bitch's face into picture frame. Somehow tonight, the whole meaning changes and connects my teeth like a bridge to this feeling of being placed reluctantly under an umbrella. I did not belong to this unknown minority. I was not an ethnic. I will not be compared to strangers who rode planes into buildings, owned bodegas or pumped gas! All I had wrong with me was this drift, and I can fix this… I swear I can fix it!

A female voice in the other room mumbled, "Isa, are you alright in there?" I had forgotten where I was and how much time had passed. You lose yourself staring into a mirror that long.

2. The Mark

"Paradise is under the feet of mothers."
– Kanz Al-Ummal, Islamic Hadith

The marionettes around me have exaggerated the rumors of my purported genius. I lost my effort to succeed around the same time I started to believe the rumors. Us ethnics get a different ending in some Queens hospital relying on a Jamaican nurse to put our respirators back in our mouths. That's the myth of how my gramps passed on—alone in a stained scrub on some August evening trying to get noticed in a hospital for throw outs. This is how we learn that we'll go out, buried the same day so the body can rest quickly, as if a quick rest is what I want. If I wanted that I would pull a Spalding Grey in the Hudson.

She chews on something, gazing through my head as if seeing some kind of vibration coming from me. "Mom, were you talking with that guy before I got here?" I say, motioning to a Chinese man in a top hat sitting near the window at the coffee shop.

"You're predisposed with race," my mother says, sipping her second cup of iced coffee. I could have sworn she was speaking with that bald Chinese man in the corner. "It's not as big a deal as you're making it out to be, really."

"Oh, so that's my problem," I say, trying to close the obligatory maternal criticism.

Cafe Kahve was a festering playhouse for South Brooklyn immigrants, mainly Exo-European Tatars and their colonized Russian counterparts, lots of unemployed welfare cheaters first-genning out in their polyester and corduroy dream worlds. As our bimonthly neutral meeting zone, it deemed a suitable place where a second-gen and her son could meet. Any other setting and she would explode on me within one hour. Worse, I would explode on her. We needed the immigrants as the buffer.

"Your problem is not your name, or your face, or your teeth," she bites into a perogi. "You've lost your hunger," she says rolling the boiled flour chunks around her mouth.

I calmly tell her, "That's the most ridiculous fucking thing I ever heard."

Mom puts down the polish dumpling.

Scratching my left arm, which has been irritating me, I tell the woman, "How am I supposed to live in a city that hates me, wants to see me fail, and—"

"I raised a whiner! You want a job, tell people your name is John or Gary or—"

"You expect me to whiten up my identity?" A couple beside us quickly looks over at me with visible awkwardness. Lowering my voice I say to her, "How far does that go? First, I tell people my name is John fucking Doe. Next minute, I'm bleaching my skin or worse—dead in the Gowanus Canal and untraceable because of my fake ID, fake skin, and then what?"

The couple leaves the shop, feeling uncomfortable. I notice the oddly placed bald Chinese man sitting behind me again. We exchange a brief glance before my mother responds.

"You have no passion. Look at you, you're a mess. You're looking all over the place like a paranoid schizophrenic."

"Do you see that Chinese guy? I think he's following me."

"My son, the head case! I don't even know what you're talking about now."

"I thought you were talking with him before I got here."

"You think you're so smart, don't you? Are you even thinking of your future? Keeping a stable job?"

"Listen, I just need ten grand for the teeth, and I'll be fine. You can live your late baby boomer life and retire with your social security. I'll live my Gen X, whatever slacker bullshit label you put on my life, and all will be fine."

"Don't turn this around again, Isa."

"You haven't done shit for me. I'm just asking for some help." The same argument we've had for years. As I spit back the conventional *this is all mommy's fault* feedback, I take notice of the circular scar on her left arm.

"Why aren't you married yet? Where are my grandchildren? You're a grown man, Isa. Grow the fuck up."

"You grow the fuck up, Mom! What was I supposed to turn into? You birthed me and tossed me into a world of worthless immigrants with no goals!" An obese elderly Russian man glances over at me slurping a bowl of borsht loudly. The bloody cabbage enters his mouth.

Mom finishes the cookie and begins taking the last sips from the cup. "You're a bastard like your dad and you have a lot to learn about asking for help. I have to go." She takes her purse and attempts to hit the exit before I can respond.

I freeze time, observing her slightly Asiatic eyes, her perfect teeth, and her rounded nose. If she was the source of my genetics, where were her genetics on me? She was oblivious to who I was. A critical eye veiled as a listener now disappearing from my broadcasts like the late rabbit on its way nowhere.

I stood up, violently shaking the table.

"It didn't occur to you that maybe I'm not exaggerating this time! That maybe something is going on!" My final cry for help fell on deaf ears, the glass door of the coffee shop slamming shut. The bald Chinese man sitting by the window grinned my way, with his pre-war era black hat and umbrella rolled tightly to perfection.

I turned around, alone, now embarrassed for flying off the handle again in public. The odd man by the window smirked and tipped his hat to me.

* * *

I left Brooklyn in 1999 thinking I would never come back, that my child-hood would be neatly tucked away in some godforsaken land, and I would gracefully continue making more than my immigrant parents. I thought one fine day when I was successful and wanted to revisit a specific pizzeria or bodega, I would have my limo take me to the old neighborhood. Then, and only then, the ghosts would return. In the dream, my older version of myself, having aged gracefully, slowly opens the limo window and observes the local block thugs. *Boy, haven't you come a long way,* I would say to myself tossing a quarter and some French fries at an Albanian kid with a weird nose. Throw a teardrop in for dramatic effect. For the most part, we all have this dream until we die in the same place, perhaps under a different illusion, sometimes dying in the same hospital we were born in, placed in a pre-purchased, one hundred percent guaranteed grave with twenty-four hour security so your soul can be assured its raft ride in heaven will be uninterrupted.

It's not my fault.

The great expectation for first generation Turkish parents is that their children become huge successes, buy them houses in New Jersey, pay for cruises, and pay back the investment placed into you growing up. What's that work out to, like five grand per Turk for a lower-middle-class family?

Here's where the problem was. I didn't see an investment in me, even emotionally, from anyone. As a child, you're told by your parents to be seen and not heard, but I've learned as an adult you're better off not seeing or hearing from them.

I looked out of the cab into the empty New York night, at empty bars and fluorescent signs, blinking only to the driver and me. Lonely drunk faces waddling through the languid streets, searching for nothing, searching for their mothers and fathers to tell them everything would be all right.

A billboard for some corporate underwear company passes us. An infertile-looking weak woman poses in ecstasy as if her brand of underwear produced happy hormones and fixed the world's ills. If I could only get my hands on that underwear, everything would be all right.

I tell the cabbie, "New York is dead at night." He coughs, ending the long silence during the ride out of Brooklyn. "Yah, we're all dead. Only a couple of weeks left."

The taxi ID says Ismail Noor, medallion number 06756. I would have said he was a fatalist last year. The year before, I would have called him apocalyptic. Before 9/11, he was a total meathead struggling like the rest of us. Tonight though, strange things fluttered through my heart. I could only believe 06756, Mr. Noor my taxi cab prophet, was reminding me about the psychic from last year who claimed I should "enjoy this Thanksgiving because it will be your last."

Doom and gloomers. Most New Yorkers had no hope left, just their little watchtowers with see-through shower doors and their little huddles. Our ethnic huddles, as precious as tons of gold and as inseparable from ourselves as our own heads. Our apocalypse movies ingrained images of broken statues and libraries under water. What happened to us after 9/11?

The taxi pulls over to a phone booth flashing a broken bulb illuminating a sign for a psychic detective. As I count the tab on my fingers, an orthodox Jewish man rushes into the subway. Ismail sucks his front teeth and watches him like a fox as he descends into the New York underground.

Disgusted, he blurts, "That man—he is devil."

I had four dollars ready for a tip, which I flipped down to three.

"Devil, huh?"

He turns back at me to see if I approve. "They want to make end of world. You know?"

I smirk and hand over the fare.

"Those are not the Jews you're looking for." I laugh, volunteering a dollar tip, reduced slowly from five for his projectile vomiting end-of-the-world spunk.

We all try to avoid the apocalypse as best we can. It's a trick we do to prevent dangling in the obvious fact that we want to die from falling meteors and fantastical floods.

I ask the cabbie, "You have kids, man?"

"Yes, two. Boy and girl, back in Pakistan." He smiles back at me, the thought of his children erasing whatever hate he was feeling for the Jews.

"We're not dead yet," I mumble opening the door. "Take care of your kids."

Damn Muslim Zombie, I think, as if my version was any better.

* * *

I stare at my reflection in a car window, one block from the bar. My hair is unkempt. My clothes are outdated and too big. I make self-deprecating critiques about my skull shape, my height, and even my walk.

My jaw line too rounded… nose too flat… lips too large… eyes, too sunk in.

The world around me begins to dissolve into the reflection, my whole being transported to age six. Standing in front of a mirror, my mother fixes the collar of a new suit I'm wearing. We both look at the reflection of me. She spits on her hand and pushes a renegade hair strand down.

"See, now you're handsome," she says.

Now I'm handsome.

In a mighty rush, within nanoseconds, my perception transforms.

Hell, I could pass as a domesticated revolutionary, even a malformed butterfly fallen out of the cocoon too early.

Out of all my mother replacements, Viki Medina was the most beautiful. She was a half dark artifact. In her head I could have been her dad, or a fantasy boy from her own childhood. Who knows? It was anything but who I was. We were another relationship based on advertisements. Billboards don't just sell underwear and cell phones; they sell subconscious lives wearing their underwear, using their technology, and maybe both.

I decide life is a series of unrelated fragments dictated by neuro-marketing companies and venture through the gold-plated doors and into the crowded bar.

Her eyes break from their miserable gaze, and she wraps around me as if I was back from a great war.

"How's my Turkish lover?"

"When are you done?" I lean back, avoiding the show of intimacy in public and suspiciously eye the clientele.

"As soon as they leave."

She was referring to the hoard of anorexic skeletons in evening dresses alongside chiseled men with coke addictions that surrounded us. A mass of the New York young rich class that could just as well be standing under the *Sociopathic Spartans on Crack (and their objectified women) Under Here* umbrella.

"Hey Isa!" she reminded me.

"What?"

"You're looking at everyone when you should be giving me a kiss."

My thoughts bounced from thinking we had nothing in common besides vociferous sexual appetites to thoughts of some bizarre wedding ceremony in an underwater Atlantis (a post-apocalyptic romance story between two *hyphenators*). Of course, I never considered the other girl's feelings. Yes, us ethnic identity freaks tend to judge ourselves by our female conquests. Ask Tayib, he'll tell you all about conquering Europe with only his penis.

When my dad found himself out of prison, he summed up his life philosophy to me over shots of Jack Daniels. I was eighteen and not much into the bar scene so having my father, who had been MIA for most of my life, bring me to one sealed the deal. I can count the number of words my dad and I exchanged. The only advice ever bestowed on me came during the one night he decided to charm his son with the best of his ethnic novelties.

"Allah judges you not by your actions..."

What the hell, I thought.

'But by the amount of women you have been with and how you dealt with them," his Turkish accent still strong.

I took a swig from my shot glass and cringed, my eyebrows furrowing as the heat singed my chest. I doubted there was anything to backup his statement, but it sunk in. Every boy wants to be told his dick is public domain.

"Ain't much of a drinker, Isa? You have to catch up!" He said, ordering another round of shots. I stared into the glass and caught a rippled reflection of my eyeball. Underneath my brain, a dendrite inside my frontal lobe applied his philosophy immediately. Fathers have enormous effects on impressionable dendrites, and ethnic ones, even more so.

I knew deep inside that when she finally saw the light, I would be the loser, the ethnic throw away you learn a lesson and move on from. Too many futile attempts in monogamy led me to see women as cheaters, manipulators, and soul-suckers. I saw myself. If I could only inject some magical love into the relationship perhaps it would last longer than one year. However, I would first need to be smacked in the face with some magic or have it removed by some.

Cheap wine is hardly magical, and tonight it would work against me.

"Cat got your tongue? Are you fasting again or something?" Viki asked.

"You're not supposed to ask whether someone is fasting. It's each person's private contract—"

"With God, huh? You got a bunch of those, don't you?"

Don't try to figure me out. Figure yourself out, I thought defensively.

"Ramadan isn't for like three months, dear. You're not supposed to ask that question anyway. It's rude." I turned to order a Jack Daniels, but keeled over from a strange pain pulsating on my left arm.

"Are you alright?" asked Viki.

I squeezed the pain spot, just outside of my upper arm. It faded away. "Fine, been having this pain in my arm. That's all."

"Um, excuse me!" Shouted one of the emotionally vacant alcohol suckers. Viki sped off to serve and inebriate.

Another emotionally vacant American, unable to make out where I'm from, gave me the once over, the twice over, and on three says, "Hey." It was the kind of hey that makes you feel like some illegal alien caught crossing over an imaginary border, her border.

I gave her my attention because mama taught me to want to be a nice Jewish boy. Processing the fact that I actually comprehended her, she paused in what seemed to be a magical white conjuration of whisky induced provocation.

"So what does *chin chin* mean in Chinese?" she asks.

Previously on my ethnic dream world, I would race through one thousand thought crystals until I hit one with the word "unharmed" a.k.a. "disaffected," right next to MILF cunt rag baby boomer racist fucktard.

"I wouldn't know what *chin chin* means in Chinese."

Startled that I could form sentences she looked around, as if the ether held a clue to the hole this pigeon lived in. "Oh, well I know *zadrovia* means cheers in Russian."

"Does it?" I asked from an imaginary psychiatrist chair charging 400 imaginary dinars an hour. The bitch doesn't quit, self-assured that I must be a total immigrant with a brain of the soon to be extinct Borneo Rhino. I was about to go crazy with thought crystal rot when I saved myself from having her projection stench.

"Listen, *chin chin* is Portuguese. I'm not sure what it means actually but some old white man who takes me out and teaches me to be civil told me I should say it to appear classy."

I was playing a game of overstimulation, too much information, give it all away in one-shot. Be quick with these bastards. She was a dumb twat but a smarter one, a trained one, won't stifle you into sarcasm.

"What?" She stared vacantly at me. I hoped the vacancy would get filled soon.

"Knock, knock!" I say.

The night dragged on. One drink followed by another. Viki serving drinks in hyper-speed as I waited tirelessly losing track of conversations watching her zig-zag around the room like a programmed bunny rabbit. Occasionally, she would stop by my stool for a kiss and let me in on what we were doing.

After seven drinks, I am given my jacket and managed to follow her outside. Viki stood at the front door wrapping around me. "Why don't we do something tonight?"

"I'm going to hail a cab," I slurred boldly, walking into the middle of street. "Give me a call sometime," I said, drunkenly smiling. She gave a sad face as light trails from passing cars fly by as I tried to focus on the yellow objects with little white lights on the signs.

"Can I at least get one more kiss?"

"How can I refuse the hottest ass on 23rd and 8th?" I said half-giggling. I hobbled back over to her and planted a wet one on her thick lips.

From my right, a crass man's voice, "Viki, isn't it a bit late to be smooching with the busboy?"

I broke from her lips. "I'm sorry. Were you just referring to me?"

"Isa, I work with him. Chill!" She whispered in my ear. He was bigger than me. Stockier too. Probably just coming to work after hitting the gym, jerking off to Asian porn and tossing on his new Kenneth Cole outfit.

He smirked. "You got something to prove to me, kid?"

Something to prove? I wondered. *Viki was probably the hottest girl any man has ever seen, and here I am locking tongues with her, and you step into our world? Yes, you son of a bitch, I do have something to prove.*

He again remarked, "Well?"

I turned to him. "Well ya' best shut your mouth and put your apron on before you get a facelift!"

Viki approached him, trying to get him into the bar. "Leave him alone, Chris. Just walk away." All I heard was her try to quell the situation as I pushed the blade out from a box-cutter in my pocket. My mental now ignited by the wrong asshole saying the wrong thing at the wrong time, three wrongs that need to be made right. The blade slid down five notches.

"Chris, just leave him alone. I'll talk to you inside," she said to him, her hands at his chest. He was still smirking at me, curious at the thought that this weird looking dude shorter than him might have more balls than him. It was the smirk of machismo that leads to drive-bys, fistfights at supermarket lines, and random acts of stress-shankings.

Why did she say to him, "Leave him alone," I thought. She has agreed with him and made me the other—a stranger.

I found myself being refrozen underneath my umbrella. Viki and Chris turning into black and white halftone images as a paranormal rain began to fall outside of my consciousness. Stuck in this mode of ethnicity, I blinked spastically trying to find reality again.

Who am I? rushed through my head like a Buddhist mantra sung in a low voice by a thousand red monks.

Mom's voice echoed in my head, *My son, the paranoid schizophrenic!*

Viki turned toward me demanding a deep stare into my wide eyes, eyes that were transfixed on pellets of raining particle hallucinations. I didn't let her try to calm me down. Chris, the overgrown interrogator, stared at the blade in my right hand as I lunged at him, pushing the girl away with my left arm. In a swoop, I slashed down with my right, just barely missing Chris' face as he stepped back. I felt an odd surge of pain in my left arm and keeled over, dropping the blade. "Fuck!" I shouted, gripping this odd pain that erupted.

"What the fuck! You're crazy man!" he screamed. Viki leapt on me, pushing me down further, so as to prevent another slashing attempt.

"Isa, calm down right now!" She stared into my eyes. My pupils dilated into oblivion unable to see what was happening. I tried to push her off while examining the strange pain. Chris scurried and shuffled, demanding Viki control the situation. I tried to keep track of where the blade fell, but the phantom pain in my left arm was throbbing intensely.

"What the hell is wrong with you?" She asked as if to wake me up from my deep freeze. I took several stunned steps away from her.

"Hey, it's alright. Come back here," she said as I tried to control myself. It was futile. The pain in my left arm was stinging. As I blinked my way back into reality, I looked at it.

At first, it was blurry.

"Baby, you alright there?"

I picked up my sleeve, revealing a mark in the shape of a circle on my left arm below my shoulder. The circle was composed of small bumps expanding and contracting like small organisms birthing yet nothing had touched me, that is, until I picked up my head again to gain focus.

I was met with a swift punch in the face that threw me off balance. Quickly, without hesitation, I cracked my neck back and regained a stance, shaking off any pain that I might have just experienced. My retinas expanded and the alcohol wore off instantly. Viki shouted "No!" As I threw my right fist upwards into Chris' mandible, his neck twisted from the velocity, making an audible cracking noise. I followed a split second afterward with a swooping left elbow to his cranium. The man collapsed backwards to the concrete. I programmatically kicked him in the rib cage with every intention of breaking his skeleton into a million shards. I threw Viki off of me multiple times, unable to hear and unable to see anything except my attacker. The last thing I remember before escaping into a cab was his ripped Kenneth Cole outfit and a blood smattered meat sack. Viki didn't even matter at that point.

3. Pigeonhole

"There are only two kinds of people in America. Those who go around calling strangers and other non-intimates by their first names and those who resent it."

– William Raspberry
Boston Globe

You learn more about people by living a lie than you do being yourself. I keep the façade up for as long as possible with whomever I think needs it. I've started to tell people I'm Italian, particularly employers. It's easier that way.

Central Asian Muslims still have a ways to go in achieving the so-called fair treatment that ethnic pluralism promises. It's at least five minutes of personal exposition with each new person.

Flash to my grandfather's picture immersed in blood and broken glass.

Veda is where high profile designers and freelance cock suckers of various skill sets go to get overpaid positions in predominantly fly by night operations. Velour Employment Destiny Agency was on the thirty-seventh floor of a building in the most polluted part of the city. Not the healthy kind of pollution either. The smell of acrid undercooked eggs hovered in the air. I sat in a pleather chair in the waiting room alongside four other tired slobs surrounded by strange Dadaist paintings and minimalist logos embossed with chrome. My sweaty hands held a yellow manila envelope, inside which was a resume of personal sales points, all overstated and glossed over with *success words*.

Two black eyes and a swollen cheek adorned my face and an underused tweed blazer was falling off my shoulders. All I could think about was the hormone laced, mass assembly line plucked fried fetuses nearby.

The clerk behind a blue tinted window called my name and smiled at me as I popped out of the chair. He lifted his fork out of a plastic container as I walked by noticing the odiferous culprit; bad salad from those bacterial buffets of sushi beside egg salads and hardened fried bananas.

I entered a cluttered cell of an office.

Her eyes scanned papers on her desk. She was my assigned headhunter and had a streak of red in her tightly pulled back hair. I noticed five earrings in one ear.

Must be a nihilist, I thought, *Good.*

"Just some advice, you should put the dates for each job on the resume."

Wrong, QC girl looking for faults.

The mark on my arm started to itch, but I resisted touching it. I might be perceived as a nervous twitching freak, possibly a meth head. Despite rubbing copious amounts of anti-fungal creams and ointments of every kind, it just got worse. Not that it mattered. She looked like the fidgety type herself, probably due to scanning peoples' holographic lies all day.

"They're all mostly contract gigs. I was staff at Morgan." I replied in modeled corpo-speak.

"And how long did you work at Morgan?" Her eyes panned up to me, the interrogation beginning. Soft brown pupils. Straight rigid jawline. An American Androidette.

"I was considered staff, but I worked for them through DevStream. That's the startup on page one."

"Right." She pauses as if to note something in her head. Her eyes turn back down to the resume. "So..." she drew out the word as if to fill in the space while she thought, "...your last real job was seven years ago, for a failed startup?"

My mark began to howl. I took the opportunity to scratch it, squirming in the process. I manage to get out a few words as I squirmed, "Page... two lists—my freelance... gigs."

She mirrored my squirm, clinching her face, and packed the resume away. "Okay, looks good. Except... most of your recent experience is independent? I see a gap from 1999 onward. You haven't worked for any company since."

"Not much of a company man, you know. Thought that was out with Reagan anyway."

I redeemed my interview posture despite her already knowing something was odd about me. I knew it too. She was flickering in and out of my perceptions, reminding me of my mother criticizing me, reminding me of the missed opportunities. Before the dream world started, I would look at people that acted like me and wonder why they were squirming, or why they were clinching their faces together. Now, I know they were reflecting me.

"Mainly freelance work under my DBA. I can provide you with the details if needed."

The details were shady.

It started with a closet full of button up shirts and ties to match, which I would coordinate based on how I wanted to feel that day. The gold tie told people I was an asset while the red shirt demanded attention. *Nine to five with plenty of overtime* was the motto until the kid with the salesman face made my knuckles settle into his eye sockets.

It wasn't my fault.

I had just graduated from college and landed that entry-level thirty thousand dollar a year gig with benefits guaranteed to every industrious young person who kept himself on the straight and narrow. It started innocently enough. Every morning I would wake up. Do as many pull-ups as I could do. Always outdoing the day before in an attempt at bettering my physicality. I would commute with the whole lot of train cars filled with the New York working class nodding off from sleep deprivation or reading newspapers. The reward being checks that rolled in every other week, which I would ritually examine to figure out how much the government took out for that week. How much of my work would be counted for when I would retire in what seemed to be an eternity away.

I became the corporation's go-to guy. They promised stock options and a promotion. High-flour lunches mixed with late night insomnia hindered my morning pull-ups and disrupted my motivation. Questions began to resound inside of me. I didn't understand how a human being could be expected to function like a worker ant on the basis of promises for the future. The secret to living this life I discovered would have to be balancing timing and faith.

Believe in the promises of the corporate world. Believe that you have followed the arrows of success. Believe you were progressing.

I would train new recruits to the company and offer them similar promises of the future.

"One day you'll be training the new guy." I said to a recent graduate and new hire. Jonathan had a plastered smile, a blue shirt, khakis, and blue eyes. I showed him the equipment, explaining what his job would be.

"These are all encoding live feeds from each of the broadcasts in studios around the country. Any questions?"

The whole time he stood, arms at his side, smiling at me too perfectly. His only question being, "So what kind of name is Isa? Is that Korean or something?"

"No," I said. The air conditioners hummed. Jonathan believed his curiosity validated a simple question. A simple question deserves a simple answer.

I said, "I'm American."

"Where are you from though?"

"So you're asking where my parents are from?" Let's just get to the point, shall we. Pigeonhole.

"Turkey. My parents are Turkish" I said, annoyed. His eyes widened and I could only guess that he hardly knew anything about Turkey, but whatever it was to him, I became it.

The Columbine school massacre fell on the same day I knocked him out. Our job was to digitally stream to the Internet every second of students being escorted out of that school. Little huddles of umbrellas labeled *Unfortunate Suburban White Kids Here* under which were bloody high schoolers. The blood came from two glitches who had decided it was judgment day and borrowed daddy's guns to play live-action *Battlefield: High School*.

It wasn't that shocking.

Lunch that day was at a table for six at the pizzeria. Jonathan and the rest of the office ants scarfed down slices and poured black water down their throats, talking about the rationale for killing classmates. Next to us a father sat with his son afflicted with Down syndrome. Jonathan took note of them and began to make a loud, obnoxious impersonation of the poor kid. The father's head resigned into his food and layers of shame and humiliation. He was trying his best to ignore Jonathan's tactless remarks.

The office ants laughed and it continued. This time he added the spectacle of making himself look retarded with ugly faces and body movements.

I felt a hot glowing pain sharply bang within my brain, like a neural storm entering full swing. My slice fell out of my hand and rapid eye movements began.

I tried to blink it away.

The laughing became static as my co-workers vanished into halftone particles.

With each blink a shift in the color of the outside world took over darkening the atmosphere into a haze and out it came from my mouth:

"Jon, you need to shut your fucking mouth!"

The laughing died down, my eyes completely glazed over. The father and his son beamed at me in a golden Technicolor while the rest of the world around me transformed into a black and white halftone.

"I'm sorry, what did you say?" Jonathan replied, up for the confrontation, a total blur to my sight. Just blue eyes.

"I think you heard me. Shut your fucking mouth." The walls of the eatery vanished and suddenly the only vision I had was his skull drenched under a cloud of black paranormal rain, a hallucination.

"Alright, Isa. Calm down, we were just having a laugh," said Greg, a nondescript ant next to Jonathan. I couldn't even perceive him. All that was present in my consciousness was an ineffable fire surrounded by ghostlike forms.

"You gonna make me?" he asked as I stood up, walking around the table towards him. My quick response attack consisted of getting into position, which I did within half a second of him asking me to *make him* stop.

I lost control, extending my arms around his head, grasping his esophagus with one of my hands and twisting his head as he reeled in shock against the wall. The ants scurried off screaming behind me. I knew I only had a short time to *make him*.

By the end of it, blood spurted from his forehead, his neck bruised with broken nose, and the prick was laid out on the floor of the restaurant. A final kick in the nuts would have been good as icing on the cake, but I was pulled up by my shoulders and thrown outside.

Finlay Shreelock was the Dean of Internal Operations for the corporation. A Yanni impersonator on the weekends, he somehow managed to do an impression of the Greek musician despite being a flaming Scottsman. Finlay also tended to order us around with that same flare that can only be described as despotic *despicitude*. Mr. Jonathan, still bleeding, smirked at me as he walked into the subsequent mediation session. Thus began the corporate evaluation.

"Isa told me what happened. Now I want to hear your side, Jonathan." Finlay spoke with his thick Scottish accent.

"I don't know. He just attacked me out of nowhere. We're just from different cultures."

What was that? Brooklyn versus New Jersey?

It may have been a childhood plagued with lowlifes. Whatever it was, I'm sure it all comes down to paying attention. People could have paid more attention to me, or I could have paid more attention to them. Mainly, I could have used some one-on-ones. Who knows? I'm an independent soul—maybe I just never listened. Instead, I created my own vices, my own good and bad. I relieved myself of the corporate world soon after opting to create my own business.

By the way, that place went belly up within a year after me leaving and nobody, including Jonathan, got any stock options.

The American Androidette hands me back the resume. She finally notices the double black-eyed injured dog in front of her, and she loses the corporate poker face for a second, probably imagining a storyline. After an eye twitch, her brief second of curiosity retracts back to android.

"Make me a copy with the dates on it and I'll send it out. We'll talk."

"Great!" I take it and place it in the manila envelope.

"So why would a hired gun like you suddenly need a full-time position?"

"Hired gun?" I laugh. "Never really thought of myself in those terms. After a certain point things change. You know what? I didn't get your name," I say to her.

"Yes, yes. Health insurance and a paycheck go a long way after twenty-five," she responds as I get up and begin walking away.

"By the way, what kind of name is Isa?"

A simple question deserves a simple answer. I turned toward her smiling like the perfect salesman.

"Jesus, in Arabic. Turkic origins." Suddenly, we were talking genetics.

"Now that's beautiful. We need more names like that here in America."

Her name never came.

4. Rifts

I feel as though I've betrayed myself and now the Cosmos wants its money back. The black eye still throbs from the swelling. The mark on my arm has entered a new stage of decay. I'm jobless, homeless, and cantankerous. I decide my best bet is to tie up loose ends, make a big change, hit the grindstone, get some payback, and find the son-of-a-bitch. Tell him what I thought of him. Step one was finding out exactly where he was.

My grandmother kneels down towards Mecca as I sit on her sofa awaiting her attention. She's on her seventy-sixth *la ilaha illallaha*, praying for the third time that day. I watched her for what seems like an eternity, repeating the mandatory praises silently. The sounds I hear are mere whispers, soft as the shapes of her supplication. *I seek refuge.* "Huwa Rahmanu r-Rahim..." *He is the merciful and the gentle.*

Rays of sunlight beam in, illuminating her blonde hair from under the thin silk head covering. I hoped she would be praying for me, the misguided American born from her son's damaged goods. I hoped her golden-haired, compassionate wisdom would be my judge and my jury all at the same time, not some fixed great eyeball that seemed to want nothing more than my surrender to it.

My grandmother finishes and rolls up her prayer rug, her back facing me. She says knowingly, "You came here to find out something."

Offering her useless grandchild some tea, or maybe engaging in some formalities, might have been a better opener but she was convinced I was conceived in vain from the day I came back from the hospital.

"What prison are they holding my father in?" I ask forcefully.

She places the rug above her head next to a stack of Qur'ans, Hadiths, and other religious texts. "Don't look for your father. You are better off."

Obviously she did not see my condition. If I was better off, I'd hate to be in bad shape.

*   *   *

Particles of light bounce back into my retina. The black tube I'm staring at emits these tiny illuminations that when arranged in moving patterns appear as images. The swollen eye shivers with tension still. This room is filled with pictures of Hollywood stars from the golden age of cinema. She snores on her mother's couch. Both of us are naked. On the wall I notice an autographed headshot of Grace Kelly flickering from the video light as if she was frozen in limbo forever.

Wasting away. I'm wasting away. This brain needs activity—a constant surge of energy. At least, that's the ploy here: push stimulation, push activity.

The information age went out of style some time between when Courtney Love's dad shot Cobain full of dope then blew his head to pieces and the Columbine massacre. Both times, America went on high self-introspection alert, asked itself some major questions about video game violence, then quickly rode out to some tropical island for spring break to get lost and hammered. America returned home to live within more car commercials and spout racial epithets at black boxes. Then came the New York date rape by Al-Qaeda. Enter Jimmy Falwell for the mass moral lecture and subsequent foreign flavored beatdowns; and here we are quickly ushered into the Android era where we all act out our mp3 fantasies and cellular dreams looking at guys like me as the enemy, while huddling in overpriced caves talking about liberation and reliving the 1980s as if *Asteroids* and laser pink knee highs are forever.

On television, a chart explaining a concept in molecular biology called *genetic drift*:

   ...*Acting on small populations, genetic drift can give rise to random se-*

lections of dominant traits. Genetic drift acts when natural selection does not, creating anomalies in the gene pool. These anomalies may give rise… unrelenting gene flow… melanin… body characteristics…

…rise in identity displacement…

I look at my arm. The strange mark surrounded by random tosses of tiny brown circles. Turks, olive skinned with brown beauty marks tracing some early genetic ancestor; a beauty mark, that strange round corpuscle referencing some far away earthly origin. Place all the marks together, multiply them by a million, and the skin turns brown. That's it. I'm a multiplication of the average randomness in a gene pool of decorated Mediterraneans. The Turk is a European, an Ethiopian, Chinese, an Egyptian, and an Arab, although the consensus would disagree. The census would still say *Other*.

A veiled Afghan woman holding her daughter staring right into the lens as a British voice describes her:

…Veiled and starved she cries for help silently living under the swift blade of fundamentalism… If only her cries could be heard, perhaps the evil that oppresses her would… that's why we here at the Christian Zionist Foundation have created a program to help women like…

I feel sick, restless, depressed. The naked girl beside me turns over and mumbles something, asleep and dreaming, I gather. She's full-blooded American, whatever that means, several generations down the pipeline. Tessa White is her name—more irony—and granddaughter of a best boy from the Hollywood studio system of the thirties. Back then, the Whites were a huge family that still kept ties with their Dublin cousins. Now here they are, nearly as disconnected from each other as I am from myself. After women's lib liberated Tessa's mom, after countless polarizing wars sent the brothers and cousins to Korea, Vietnam, and the bible belt; after the hippies, yuppies, and mythological American guppies came home to roost, there was no connection besides Tessa, her mom, and the Arlo Guthrie look-a-like boyfriend. The White family was now small, but their Victorian home was huge with all the amenities of a well-assimilated bunch of immigrants and decorated with the prizes of Grandpa White's life: autographed pictures, props, musical sheets. Walking through the house was a safari through memories from Hollywood's golden years. A person could lose himself.

"Beware the bald Chinese man!" She yells in her sleep, waking up wide-eyed. My mark began to howl.

Her breathing was hard.

"You were dreaming. Go back to sleep," I said, itching my arm.

"I was dreaming? Oh." Slightly displaced she pulls me in for a reassuring kiss pushing my full lips against her thin ones.

I resisted. "Go back to sleep, there are no bald Chinese men here, silly."

The odd mark had gotten worse.

"That was strange. I saw this giant man standing over you, and you were huddled in a corner crying."

"Was I?" I asked, laughing as she took notice that the mark worsened.

"Doesn't look so good, that thing." She said, drifting back into dream state.

"Yeah, I should get it looked at."

The Afghan show cut to the green video of Marines kicking open a farm door and pointing their guns at a group of children. "Where are the terrorists?" they demanded as the kids held each other close, staring into the shaft of titanium rifles. I turned it off as she began to snore lightly, tired from a night of multiple orgasms. The sound of my cell phone told me a text message had arrived.

Let's get together mañana, Nooner, Viki xxooxx

I examine my mark in the bathroom mirror. It had become severe, resembling a cigar burn or branding of some kind. I touched the dry patch of flaky skin, watching bits of myself fall into the sink. *Tomorrow I'll go to the clinic.* I grab the ointment but catch a glimpse of myself in the mirror.

You're getting old, Isa, I say to myself. *Got to get moving. It's all in your head.*

I smile insanely wide in order to get a view of that damn tooth, the protruder. It juts out abnormally, still showing no signs of natural regression. The moment bursts. Minions for the gods of alienation march towards the horizon of my consciousness. I witness, as if for the first time, my skull, my eyes, my mark. Waves of who I am attack in thought explosions. Neural storms.

So what kind of name is…?

Fists fly through the air hitting their shadowy targets in cadenced bursts, one after another. I blink to come back but it's already begun.

I dream, walking through life in the distance; never able to see the person I am trying to figure out. When he appeared, albeit in flashes, I hoped to see myself, but I could not claim this dream. I was witnessing another man's life in hyperspeed like a time-lapse camera placed overhead throughout a lifetime. This was certainly not me. This man had curly hair, like an Egyptian. Perhaps a fiber optic connection to one of the beauty marks resonating in dream space. He wore blue shirts and tucked them in. His face stayed elusive, playing dream games with me, always appearing as the back of his head. He would turn around to yell at his American wife, but his head was always backwards. I saw him running around living two lives, one in Egypt with one family and set of rules and another here in American with another wife.

This wasn't me at all.

I am forced to watch this *nowhere man*'s life, his multiple wives, his reactionary temperament, and ultimately his burial surrounded by shrouded eyes in a colonized society—his tombstone was one word, *Inoculate.*

I began dreaming my teeth falling out again. Screams echoed as each one dropped into the sink. *It's only a dream* whispered in my ear as I tried to scavenge at a neverending deluge of teeth. I grabbed my ear as if to grab the voice and off it came. My ear pulled off like a piece of putty.

Maximum effort is the only way to transformation.

I looked at my ear in my right hand crawling with ants. When suddenly I was aware of the dream, awake inside of it with the ability to move freely. I turned toward the invisible voice and asked, *Who are you?*

It responded, *Who are you?*

Now I'm eight years old strapped into the passenger seat of my shadowy stepdad's Toyota mini-van. I'm still aware but no longer in control of the dream. This is a real memory playing out exactly as it did that day. His lanky emaciated figure enters the driver side holding a bag with my mother's wedding ring inside. *Get me out of here,* I try to take control—break the memory, *I do not need to see this!*

He takes out a vial of coke and unscrews the top as my tiny self watches. A tinier spoon is connected to the lid as he lifts a bump out of the vial. About to snort it, he realizes I'm beside him and extends the spoon to me.

Stop!

"You want some?" He asks with blue eyes gazing into mine. Either he was so high I seemed like a buddy, or he was actually offering an eight-year-old stepson a bump of blow.

"No," I said just like when it happened.

Flash to the cabdriver from the other night, "That man, he is devil!"

Without hesitation he inhaled the powdery contents of the spoon and quickly hustled the paraphernalia into his pocket. Then something happened.

An event that was not part of the original memory—his face would change into my current adult face. Now I was in two bodies, and I physically felt the dream control come back.

"Your mom is going to like this ring," I said as though reading a script. I put the car in drive, snorting the recedes up into my sinuses. "We're going to be a happy family."

Suddenly, I was in control again. Driving yet simultaneously an eight year old watching that same driver. Two sets of decisions from two minds of the same person became evident. My dream world was a duality. The younger self reacted like a demon child roaring incessantly.

"Why did you do that to me?" I asked myself, leaping violently onto the older me. A battle of the selves ensued. I could not control the controllers at this point. The driver attempted to keep the car on the road but the blow kicked in so hard. Streets became strands of streaking light. The inner-child wrestling the driver's neck, making guttural screams. "How many more mistakes do we have to make?"

"Get off! I can't control it!" the driving-self said. "We're still young. We still have time!"

The inner-child blocked my line of sight and threw his head into mine, screaming like demon spawn, "There is no time!"

"Move! We're gonna hit…"

The last thing we saw before the car spun out of control was a figure in front of the car dressed in all black wearing a top hat. It was the Chinese man, holding an umbrella and smiling at me. The top of the umbrella was odd—like a syringe.

Crash. Black.

All I heard was Tessa's voice. "What's your problem, Isa?" My eyes blinked open slowly as I discovered I had collapsed on the bathroom floor.

"I must have had a flashback." Pushing myself back up, I downplayed the situation, smiling as I met her eye level. "Why are you laughing? Stop laughing," she said.

"My central nervous system hasn't been the same since that codeine overdose," I said.

"What the fuck are you talking about? Explain this text message!" She held my cell phone up with Viki's booty call prominently displayed. Rubbing my neck, it appeared this particular façade was over." Come on Tess. I'm freaking out here, and you're going on about some—"

"Quit your bullshit. You're seeing someone else?" She questioned.

"I'm having a real hard time here, and I wish you would just—"

She hustled my hoodie out from under the pillows and threw it at me. "Get out of my house, Isa. You're a sniveling little creep."

I pushed her aside and grabbed my pants from the other room. "So you want to play that game? I can play that fucking game too."

"Oh, that's it. This is a fucking game to you? You think you can just use people."

I threw on my shirt, feeling the pain on my left arm still humming and periodic traces of the waking dream I just had. That man whose face I never got to see. How he lived these two lives, his second life being as a partially hydrogenated American.

"You want to talk about using people? Look at you, pathetic little girl. You have everything—a home, a future, an uninterrupted existence," I said.

"Stop making excuses for being a slut. That's all you are!"

"Oh, I'm a slut now? You're fucking sleeping with the enemy, and I'm a slut?"

"Don't flip this, Isa. You're the one sleeping around, and your exotic self-important nonsense is getting old!"

I wrestled my phone out of her hand managing to make her fall in the interim cracking open the tiny circuitry. She burst into tears holding half of a newly broken phone.

"Get the hell out of my life!" She decreed in between sobs. I foraged for phone parts assembling it back into working shape.

I heard her yell as I ran out in the Brooklyn night, "If you think you're the enemy, you'll always be the enemy!" Rain poured down as if some great weatherman was trying to dig his dramatic point into me. Deep under my dark heart in my heart of hearts, I knew she was right.

5. Alienated

I wander the streets and sleep on trains. A shady saint smells up the train cars bantering about all kinds of drunken observations. His leather-faced wisdom beckons snarls of disgust from straphangers. A business mind becomes an uber-borealis all-encompassing takeover of blues and grays, stretch pants, silvery long sleeves with v-necks. A supreme minimalist form of proto-man, career-based, like a blank white canvas that sells for millions because the artist has made a sleek important statement. I sit on rocks by the abandoned beach, shivering under my hood. New York has a way of taking handfuls of sand and separating each granule into it's own cocoon.

An invisible social architect, who presumes an identity upon them, divides one from the other. I can try to keep these presumptions away and only focus on the great handful handled by the omniscient maker of the sand itself. The labels still remain. I'm starting to believe the City Planning division in cahoots with Johnson & Johnson has far greater power than the deified reason for creation. Together they are responsible for the assumptions both being made on me by the world and from me towards the world. I need to escape.

"Do you speak English?" the court appointed attorney says. I stand on trial for too complex of a name. I stand here in these courtrooms, at first adamantly in defense of myself, but as time goes on, less and less interested in a defense of my roots of my existence. The plutocracy forces forgetfulness. Plus, what is the root of my existence anyway. These ethnic labels we assume onto one another are but delusions we apply to our little huddles. We ignore the alienation of this post-post-modern pre-apocalyptic world. In the end, no matter Turk, heathen, or Jew, we are alone. That's a hard lesson to teach, and I've learned it, thanks to fourteen Saudi hijackers. Thank you, Grand Emir Abdullah. How many more me's are out there?

For all it's worth, I fear forgetting what this place does to a person. I fear I may start believing this is who I am, and the presumptions are all true. But tonight I sleep somewhere between the rocks and the hard places in between.

Outside the bus window, fog-drenched faces pass by reflecting into my sleep deprived hooded eye. I keep telling myself these faces have nothing to do with gene pools and ancestry. We are all the same bodies bumping our way to a place of solace or grief or limbo. These faces, like granules of unsorted sand, reflect in my hooded reflection, and none of them are comparatively superior to the next. We are all oppressed.

Oppressed by what?

My cell rings a broken dirge. The LED screen cracked and sandy says *Unknown Call*.

"Yeah."

"Mr. Demirayak?" His voice shook as he attempted to pronounce it.

"Who's this?"

"Am I pronouncing your name correctly?"

The question initiated a slight blurring of my vision. No. Obviously you're not if you have to ask. "Depends on who you are. Make it quick, my cell is on the fritz."

"It's your cells that are on the fritz, Isa. Complicated names have complicated lives, don't they, Mr. Demirayak."

"Who the fuck is this?"

"Let me introduce myself. My name is Tom Wishery. I represent a headhunter agency in Washington and we were forwarded your resume from Veda."

That nihilist bitch from the agency actually did something for me. "Oh—from Veda, right."

"Well Mr. Demirayak, I have a very well-known technology client who is looking for a candidate willing to travel."

"I'm sorry, who are you again? I'm on the bus right now, sort of in between things."

His voice was coming in and out of signal. I slammed the phone against the seat in front of me as if to initiate a quick repair. The man sitting there looked back at me, annoyed, as I took the phone back to my ear hearing, "Would that be something you would be interested in? Escape, money, and a position?"

"I'm sorry, what exactly are you talking about? Who are you?"

"Mr. Demirayak, I can't give out much information over the phone. I'd like to set up a meeting with you. I'll be in the city later today. Is four o'clock good?"

The old lady sitting beside me sighed, indicating this conversation had gone too long. "What's the pay?" I ask the strange voice.

"Meet me in the café of the megastore on 42nd street tomorrow at ten. I'll be with a partner wearing sunglasses.

"Hold on, what exactly is the job for? Will you be wearing the glasses or will your—"

"See you at four, Mr. Demirayak."

Click. My cell completely dies.

Five Killed in Turkish Suicide Bombing reads a headline that the man in front of me is reading. His burly head shakes in disbelief as he murmurs, "Fuckin' terrorists." I should keep my lips sealed. Say as little as possible and just get to the clinic and get this mark looked at. I should do a lot of things.

"Buddy. Turks aren't the terrorists." I say, leaning up behind him. Startled, he turns back as I continue feeling some odd desire to right wrongs. "I bet that bombing was done by Kurdish rebel forces against the Turks. Totally different than the London bombings."

I had broken the unwritten New York seal of silence for discussions of terrorism on public transportation, but it wasn't my fault. *None of this was my fault.* I had been wandering the streets in a post-traumatic state of nowhere all night. I managed to fall asleep on the beach after I left Tess's, where I had more hallucinations and flashbacks revolving around my own growing psychoses. I knew something strange was happening. I sat on rocks, keeping myself warm by huddling underneath my hoodie. The cold seawater shook the moon's reflection, distorting it. Motion of white streaking waves reminded me that perception is a bitch. Everyone gets it wrong. Tell a child an untruth and change his whole perception. The moon wobbled in these reflective liquid rifts. I tried to cleanse my mind and perceive nothing. If there was no heaven or hell just the thinking that made it so, I was going to change my thinking. Simply meditating on murky Coney Island water was not enough to do it though, as an insidious pain from the mark on my left arm pulsed. The sun rose and my fragmented journey continued out of the night onto this bus. This morning was simply an extension of an ongoing nightmare.

"Oh yeah?" The union jack in front of me was interrupted by my comment. His middle-aged stare was a scope, and I was the target to a mustache covering a coarse mouth with an ever-coarser tone.

Fate concludes you are the universe and you are everything you can possibly be. The idea is that the suffering is part of the plan. A plan that also includes the oppressor as the thing that makes you suffer. If I am taking things in at the rate that I should be taking them in, and my own oppression is predestined, where the fuck does that leave me?

"If you don't mind me asking," he grunts. I knew what was coming,

"Where are you from?" Emphasis on the *you.*

"Listen, I was just telling you what's going on. Forget I said anything."

The old lady nearby peered at me with a suspicious eye. Tess echoed in my head, *You'll always be the enemy!*

"You don't know what's happening kid. *Fucking terrorists* doesn't mean I was talking about the Turks…" He wasn't a bad guy, I just read him wrong. Why can't I think straight—sleep deprivation, the cold, hold on, is it cold? I'm sweating under this hoodie, under the thermal sweater where bits of the odd wound break off… decaying. I can recall looking in the mirror yesterday, or was it the day before? The bus rides by New York's prison zone of subsidized housing a.k.a. the projects. *All aboard to the land of alienated strangers!* Around me, the hordes of them were just looking at the strangest of them all—this dirty lowlife. Never mind the Puerto Rican couple on methadone drooling on themselves. Look mommy. Look daddy. Look at your son—more educated than you, the second-genner. Things were supposed to be better.

I could look back and say that at least my real dad wasn't a lowlife, but the fact was everyone was a lowlife. The terror came from feeling adults were so misled. I would one day become the most misled. I was awake in the childhood dream, thinking and breathing. Making assessments of what a particular episode would do to modify my lifelong behavior patterns. I grew to allow experience to do with me what it chose.

Or did I choose? After repeated trauma in one way or another, everything is traumatic. It becomes a familiar taste of self-destruction, a flavor that tastes like I chose it. I chose to be traumatized.

"I'm not a terrorist! Stop looking at me that way!" I yelled out. The succession of events was too much. I felt a rush of *alienated stranger craziness* soak in as the color dropped out—black and white halftones of body forms around me staring. The bus was now a sealed vacuum of my personal hell as I hobbled up from seat to seat, grabbing people's shoulders through the crowd, rambling like a madman.

"America's fighting a war on terror? We're fighting this war? You versus me versus you. Is that it? Oh, look at Afghanistan. Look at Saddam. Hello! Look at yourselves. What about right here in America? 290 women are brutally raped with a forty mile radius every second—not by Arab men.

There's a bigger war to fight people. On our own soil…"

My stomach rumbled. My mark howled. I keeled over, nauseous, holding my stomach. Commuters were trying not to pay attention to the crazy sickly kid with the dark circles. However, they couldn't help but listen. Someone tried to elbow me away and whispered to me, "Didn't your mother teach you how to behave?"

I managed to squeeze out an ineffectual synthesis of the lecture.

"…and for some reason I'm the terrorist! I'm not a damn tourist! I was born in this country!"

The bus pulled up to the clinic. The burly man stood up. I couldn't make him out at first, but as he fixed his top hat, pushing through the crowd, his hand reaching for something from within a tightly wrapped trench coat, I realized it was the Chinese man. He rushed through the passengers and grabbed my arm injecting me with a needle, "Isa Demirayak, it's time to come with me. You've fallen behind."

6. Wanted

"If there is a class which has nothing to lose but its chains, the chains that bind it are self-imposed, sacred obligations which appear as objective realities with all the force of a neurotic delusion."

Norman Brown
Life against Death: The Psychoanalytical Meaning of History

"They don't use the same needles anymore, but in the sixties and seventies, the immunization shots were applied by a super-needle…" The emergency room doctor chips away at my mark with a tongue suppressor, "…usually on this exact spot." Odd scars cover Dr. Delgado's fingertips that lead inexplicably up his hand and under his lab coat.

"You know—foreigners, immigrants, aliens…"

He's Spanish I bet. His ID card says Jose Delgado. "I get it," I say interrupting his racist synonyms. "It's not a shot. I was born here. No way, it can be any kind of shot. See I was in a fight, and it just started…" my speech was slurring and the hospital lights were creating spiraling motion trails around me.

"Oh, were you?" He asks with a tone I had heard Tessa have the night before upon discovering Viki's text message. He looks straight at me. His eyes analyze my skull shape, breaking down my lineage bone by bone. I sneer and rub my nostrils up in an attempt to break his bizarre focus on my jaw line.

"...fall behind." I blurt out.

"No. We don't fall behind here, Isa. We're doctors. We run ahead to progress," Delgado responds, tapping particles of skin into a petri dish.

"Well?" I ask, still waiting for a diagnosis as his eyebrows lift up like he's having an epiphany. For some reason, I am becoming weaker by the second. I remembered my mom and dad had scars in the same location from getting the shots in question, but the memory faded as the pain increased. "Is there anything I can do to relieve the pain right now? Drugs, antibiotics?"

"Can't be too sure. I'm not a dermatologist. You need to see a specialist, but I don't think you'll have much time for that." He turned away and merged back into the infected mass. I squinted into the distance, watching him fade into a crowd of color. Hardly making out any detail, I do manage to notice a Japanese woman in the bed across from mine caressing her stomach. The dirty and haggard lady was probably homeless. She looks up and smiles. The emergency room fluorescents shine on her, revealing no front teeth and what seemed to be dark scars on her face—like the ones on Dr. Delgado's arms. These people have the *Scarred Up Motherfuckers Under Here* umbrella hanging over all of them. I refuse to be a member of this leper huddle. "Get me out of here," I say, trying to find the energy to prop myself up. A hand from someone I cannot make out throws me back down on the bed.

Delgado appears again with new medical paraphernalia. "I've never seen anything quite like this. Dermatitis. Basal cell carcinoma. Those are common." Something about him doesn't seem sincere.

Where had he just gone? I wondered.

He lifts a strand of dying skin. "However, this is different. There's an indication of necrosis on the underlying epidermal..." The flap of skin falls off, and we watch it float gently to the ground together.

I sit on the edge of the rolling bed in an emergency room filled with screaming old people and the vagrantly infected mass. My consciousness is fading, my skin is shedding, and I can barely make out his assessment.

"Necrosis? Is my skin dead?"

He kicks the disembodied sliver of flesh under the bed. "Partially dead. I mean you're still alive, right?" Laughing, he peers in with a magnifying glass and light. "Could be worse. You could be imagining all of this. You ethnics tend to have somaform disorder."

"What?" I say, taken aback. "I'm not et...nik."

"See that lady over there?" Delgado points to her.

The Japanese lady resembles a distant Central Asian relative. Her mouth begins to form a silent word.

"Comes in everyday," Delgado says, "Thinks there's a dead baby in her stomach." He was edgy now, his eyes appeared exaggerated and large through scratched up bifocals probably from working long hours in this emergency room inspecting wounds and infections all day—or was it something else? Why was a nurse preparing some solution beside him?

The doctor had mysteriously greeted me as I entered the clinic as if waiting for me to arrive. I begin to get suspicious. Why can't I remember how I got here? "Don't you need my next of kin, or guardian information?"

"Judging from the way you look, I don't think anyone cares about you, regardless," Delgado responds. The nurse laughs, and a voice behind me grunts.

"Funny," I say, still eyeing my only genetic neighbor in the room—the homeless lady. I realize my preoccupation with the Chinese might be tied into a long lost genetic memory. Turks, after all, are Central Asian.

He places the light back into his pocket, leaning into me. "You alright, son?"

I continued squinting. Dizzy.

Then I lock onto her lip movements. She was mouthing over and over again the phrase, "Not—a —doctor, not—a—doctor." I try to prop myself up again.

Delgado catches the communication and throws me down horizontal. "You don't look well, Isa."

As my head hits the cot, my vision fractures into halftones. "Fuck. Not another episode."

"Maybe we should run some standard tests."

"Get your hands off of me!" I yell. His body weight resting on my chest, the doctor signals to the nurse ,who shuts the curtains around the woman.

"I'm fine," I say struggling to get back up, "just having these strange dreams. It's all in my head… now let go. This isn't helping!"

"What's in your head?" He pressed down more aggressively.

Screams resounded from within the Japanese woman's curtained bed. They're sedating the poor woman for talking to me. What have I gotten myself into? The pain in my arm is so profoundly distracting my mind begins to drift.

"The dreams. Visions. I'm in between things. The mark. Dad said it was like an ethnic shot from the sixties… I have to go—you're not a doctor."

"Your dad didn't say anything. I told you that. These dreams are they triggered by…"

This bizarre doctor is suppressing me. The world shifts to black and white. My pupils dilate. "You're making me angry, doc," I say, barely able to keep my eyes open. The room turns into charcoal-like halftone pixels leaving only Delgado's face in the form of some blue-eyed devil fidgeting with something in his pocket.

He mumbles something but all I hear is, "…feeling like a fall behind."

I use all my power in an attempt to throw him off when suddenly my arms are strapped down by shadow figures. My perception is so scattered, the doctor's face is all I can reasonably decipher, but it's not even his face. I cannot make anything out.

"No, when I was a kid, my dad said—" I push myself back up a final time.

"Right Mr. Demirayak. Your dad. Your dad never existed, now get down." I am rocked back horizontal again and begin moaning words I can't fully organize.

I shake my head back and forth saying words in no order. "The dad said my mark was a girl… I have to tourist the towers, and she… was a fasting in the rain… by the rocks."

"One gets the mark after many episodes, not just one, and you, Mr. Demirayak, have passed the point of no return." I scream to conjure up a final blast of adrenaline into my body, but the shadows increase their power gripping me down like taming a wild elephant. The doctor pulls a needle, shoots up some of the liquid and says, "Consider yourself—inoculated—Mr. Demirayak"

He forcibly injects me directly in the middle of the mark. I try to resist, but the pain is astounding.

I release a powerful last scream, my back contorting as the medication rushes into my blood. My trademark quick attack spasm reaction was not working. I was short-circuiting. These fucking colonists were mentally raping me.

"What's the hurry? We've been waiting for longer than you can imagine." He turns back to his other cronies and orders to initiate a transfer.

My body relaxes into anesthetic bliss as the shadows release their grip, telling Delgado, "He's almost out."

The Doctor turns to me. "Oh, the great American experiment can lead to so many variables. People born in different places need control, a sense of purpose."

What was he talking about? I manage to get out one last breath, "But I was born—"

Just then my eyes roll back into my head as everything goes dark. Thunderous echoes from people yelling at each other to grab me, keep me alive, and get me somewhere. Flash. I take a second to breathe. Blast. Thoughts of the past envelop me like rising smoke continuing to mutate my awareness. Broken glass, the past, talking to myself in the mirrors of bathrooms, burned pictures… and then for a moment, I opened my eyes. There he was. Walking alongside the bed looking at me—the bald Chinese man wearing a top hat.

"Who are you?" he queried in military debriefing talk while moving quickly next to my horizontal body.

I could hardly form words. "Fuck… you," I sludge out rolling down what felt like a long ramp, bright lights and faces all around me.

"Do you know what day today is?" About to give another great defiant response I drifted again, eyes rolling around for a moment before going back into the darkness. It was like dying. Waking up. Dying and waking up again.

It occurred to me in the darkness of my own mind that someone somewhere right now is having a relatively normal existence. That person, probably upstate or in the country, watches television and occasionally reads a small book. The book is a popular one bought by huddles of "normal" people.

Collectively, I realize, they are not concerned with my preoccupations at all. This ongoing narrative of my last few weeks on the planet is without function to them. They cannot value my hallucinations—my dream world for their attention lies solely in the strange distractions of our time that will inevitably wash up in another time and be regarded as our golden cows. I am but a blip on the map of their idea of the "rest of the country." A first-generation, self-professed stranger in a strange land, founded on a premise of diversity under an Anglican God that tells the perennial "them" to stay subdued for they are saving the universe and need full cooperation. However, we are "they" now. We've drunk from the wine of self-hate they created for us. Complete with the tang of worthlessness, but working for their golden cow. I was brought here through my parents being brought here through wars that displaced millions of people from millions of homelands to eventually end up in one great homeland blessed supposedly by a strange deity who's only trinity is technology, economy, and corporation.

The last thing I hear is, "Today is your birthday, Judd. Happy birthday."

7. Reset

> *"Ethnicity' is an anti-concept, used as a disguise for the word 'racism'— and it has no clearly definable meaning ... The term 'ethnicity' stresses the traditional, rather than the physiological characteristics of a group, such as language—but physiology, i.e., race, is involved ... So the advocacy of 'ethnicity,' means racism plus tradition—i.e., racism plus conformity— i.e., racism plus staleness."*
>
> – Ayn Rand, "Global Balkanization"
> *The Voice of Reason*

The picture was the first thing that came into focus. A medium-sized frame with the silhouettes of a couple. Chrome blazed ornamentation decorated the frame, a brief shine reflecting at me. More things came into focus. What a restful sleep. I stretch out, realizing failure was reserved for thugs and ethnics. Secondhand for second-rates. Not me. No, no. As I lift myself off a sofa,

I feel like I am entitled to everything. No longer felt like a seeker. I am a finder—the found man. That seeker was someone else.

Hold on…

The chrome frame is mine. This $1,000 chair that I'm waking up in is mine too. I rub my eyes to get a better view. It's also me but this woman, though, who is she?

"Happy birthday!" She shouts, popping in front of the picture of us replacing her two-dimensional face with her real one.

Of course, Diana, I always forget, *my precious college sweetheart,* I think in an unfamiliar voice.

"You remembered," I say. Her familiar face illuminated, as usual, shining at me with the new morning light.

"How can I forget the day we met, babes?" She says.

"Oh, right," I say, a sense of agreeability coming over me, crushing a nanosecond of imagined dread.

"That was strange," I say, examining Diana's sharp profile and perfect features as she walks to the door, expecting me to follow.

"What was strange, honey?"

"Nothing, I had this feeling," I say, walking over to the window, feeling present centered, feeling—shall I say, perfect.

"But I feel great, babes." The distorted reflection of someone else hits me from the window where mine should be. Fleetingly, I accept it as my own with no objection.

"Okay, hurry up, everyone is waiting for you," she says opening the door.

I look outside. The view is amazing. From where I was I could see all of Central Park from 59th street to Spanish Harlem. "The little granules of sand. All the tourists, look at all the tourists," I whisper to myself.

"Hey, hon," I say. "Yes, dear?" She says from the doorway. "I love you," I say.

She laughs and replies, "I love you too, now come on, you have some surprise guests!" Diana exits the room. I look down at both my arms, examining them, brushing off any lint from the nap. I lift my sleeves. My arms are in perfect shape, toned and muscular. I look at my diamond gilded watch, 12:02 p.m., September 11th, 2001, *Four ones and three zeros,* I think. "Now that's a clever looking set of digits." Seems significant for more than being my birth-day. "It's like a mirror of itself," I say out loud, entering the next room.

"Happy birthday!" The crowd yells.

"What's like a mirror of itself?" asks Diana with an odd scientific ur-gency, whispering in my ear. In front of me is a room full of my closest friends and family. I lean to my wife. "You caught me talking to myself again." Person after person kisses me, shakes my hand and pats me on the back.

"Son, happy thirtieth!"

"There he is!" I exclaim. "You flew in just for this?" I ask his Viking ex-pression now relaxed like the warm father who slept alongside me when I feared monsters under the bed—my noble comforter, my first myth.

"I wanted to be here to mark the beginning of your aging gracefully," he said in jest.

We all laughed. Diana announced, "Speak for yourself Daniel, Judd will never age. He still looks as young as the day I met him."

Yes, I remember that night. "Thank God you left your bag at that bar."

On the walls of the room were Diana's doctorate in psychiatry degrees and various awards, for… wait, what did I do again? Something didn't feel right, like today something big was going to happen.

"Chin Chin!"

Glasses in the air clanging together. The smell of champagne and the sound of celebration continue, but an odd sense of urgency overtakes me. "This has all been so overwhelming, and I'm thrilled everyone made it." They listen to me intently. "If you would all excuse me for a moment, I would like to freshen up."

I walk into the bathroom and lock the door behind me.

I examine myself in the mirror, clenching my teeth together and smiling wide to get a view of… wait. I look perfectly sane. The teeth glimmer. Their symmetry is the ultimate Jerry Seinfeld salesman's smile.

I lift my hands to my face as if seeing it for the first time, running my fin-gers across the straight line from my forehead to the tip of a perfect nose. Forcing my right eye open, I examine a bright hazel pupil with the other eye. They were shapes like rigid square rectangles in an American Cowboy skull.

Haven't I seen this face before? It is, after all, my own, right?

I pinch the skin on my right cheek above the cheekbone pulling it away from the bone. I grab the other side trying to pull the tight skin to feel something, anything. A sensation was there, that I can attest, but the feeling of this off-pink-colored skin lacked a certain texture. The mirror reflected back the image of someone I felt was myself but not, a strange conflict of emotion rushing through my lymph nodes, cells carrying some residue of an unlearned emotion.

A spark in my head ignites. I examine myself in the mirror, slowly pressing my fingernails harder against my face. I recall the residue, but I can't place the unlearned emotion. My hand digs into the skin deeper, the layers of epidermis compressing, changing from the piggish tint it was to bright red, the veins cracking under the pressure.

The fingernail on my pointer presses through my face now, puncturing the outer layer. Blood begins to drip from the new wound.

"Aahhh!" I shout with a raspy gnarling gurgle. The pain is extreme but does not matter. My left hand pierces a fistful of skin, tearing it slowly from the muscle on my skull.

Splashes of blood pop out from under the exposed skin creating new blotches on the mirror.

"Judd, open this door right now!" insist the sounds of my so-called father and wife.

Spots of blood over spots of blood over spots of blood, my hands peeling off each side of my face. *One of these kids doesn't belong here, one of these kids is not the same, which of these kids doesn't belong here… plug him up, and drain his brain.*

The mirror reflection is now drenched by blood splatters under which it shows me my exposed eye muscles and the retina it once protected. A throbbing, burning layer of facial tissue—skin partially ripped off dangling from a once conquering mug.

The sounds from outside the bathroom increase, "Judd, open this door or we're…"

The razorblade I grabbed seemed conveniently placed, like the red wire on a ticking bomb. I went right for the cheekbones with it, digging the blade in near my right eye and going through to the muscle fiber, slicing downwards.

"This is what I call roman cheekbones," I muttered as arteries tossed nodules of blood around me.

Then a loud thud, the bathroom door exploded open revealing the phonies—the actors of my new life, now exposed for who they really were. They were horrified at the sight of me. Smiling back at them, I took a final slash from the left cheekbone, splashing onto the stunned likenesses of a family terrified as they watched muscles on my face detach, coming apart at the fiber like snapping rubber bands, parts flung by the momentum, hitting them. Diana fainted as a chunk of my jaw muscle flew off and grazed her own jaw.

When I was a little oaf of sorts, my father told me not to look in the mirror too much. "The Devil will take you over," he used to say. I was never frightened by the prospect of being taken over by anything, let alone the hellish character. Besides, the "mirror," as referred, was not much of a conscious thought. The mirror did not exist.

As I fall to the floor, prostrate in a pool of blood and human tissue, my skull exposed with strands of cut muscle hanging on only by the plasma adhesive between the bone and flesh, my last vision is that of the skinned skull of a man I never knew—now without lips so his bare blood soaked teeth was the perfect salesman's face, looking back at me like Narcissus and the lake.

From a child's perspective, there was no purpose for a reflection—none whatsoever. Until this final moment, my last vision, I remembered after all of these years; my mother licked her palm and put down a renegade hair strand telling me, "There, now you are handsome!"

I thought, "Wow. I'm handsome." Finally.

HALAL PORK

Soup

The Battle of Arabia was past deadline and billions of sheckels over budget. We were overbooked and underpaid, and I was thirsty. My armored camel lay dead on the straights of Horus, inches from the only fresh water in (insert exotic Middle Eastern city loaded with post-apocalyptic media references, i.e., use the suffix –istan after any word). I crawled over sand for what seemed like eternity. The rays of the burning sun held back by my Turfscab, a new line of Turban-scarf-veil-hijab's for men (made by Armani). Oh, these last steps towards Olivia were the toughest of all. Atop an oddly placed sea vessel near the desert's end, my muse awaited her Saracen hero.

"'Tis I, Lady O–livia!"

We squinted at each other. "Shah Jehan, you've returned!" Here is where paradise begins, and the hell of war ends in the arms of my fair lady. Fighting off the Infidel forces with their domesticated dragon warfare was not as easy as the flyers advertised, partly due to a spelling error on the part of the typist.

JOIN THE JEEHAD
Winners get bitches!
P.S. The Nordic forces will collapse upon seeing our shower of
mighty taqwaforce weaponry. Don't fret. Show up to the showers at
44 Outer Quatrian, Kafir City. B.Y.O.Q.

Sure, you always get told one thing but have to contend with some unforeseen circumstance that screws your plan up. There was no weaponry or even technology in the Arabian war chest. There was no shower of power; a man was lucky if he even got a slingshot. When I enlisted, I would get a wooden spear and a one-legged camel with flimsy chainmail named Barbaros. We managed to hold our own, guarding the straight until those damn unforeseen circumstances began. I'm unfit to recall the outcome of the battle or even if there was any enemy force. Even as I approach my darling in these final moments of my war career, I wonder what Nordic forces look like. To my recollection, the stories are a mushy soup of badly trimmed mustaches and long waits for port-a-potty caravans. I vaguely recall something about a golden pig and a cow that stood erect. Together they protect the secrets of immortality, which according to a certain mad Imam, resides within the hooves of the pig and the opposable phalange of the humanoid cow, but the details elude me.

I was just in it for the women and loot—none of which I found. With a breath of exaltation, I voraciously tore off my Turfscab revealing a snazzy leisure suit, magically snapping a hat to match and flicking it on my head. Jehan had returned with the soup. Hold on—soup?

The black and white film of this fantasy jams in the projector.

"Soup?" Olivia asked, the pitch of the audio track warbling. S—O—W—U—P

Hold on, hold on. Where am I again? Pay attention.

"And that's how you make lentil soup."

Barbaros, my boss at Kaffir Buerger, slammed the aluminum lid down on the soup cauldron. He was a short older man wearing a blue outfit to indicate his managerial status. It was mandatory at Kaffir Buerger that employees wore identical outfits to Barbaros with the exception that employees (me) had to garb the hat. I hated the hat, a floppy rubber pig wearing a kufi.

"So hold on a second," the pig on my head bouncing, "if a lentil is not a bean, what is it?"

"A leg–ume! I told you a million times already! It's a legume! Now go impale those shish kebabs."

"Where are the impalers again?"

"How many times do I need to tell you?"

"Just once, sir."

A customer briskly walks in. "Salaam-alaikum brothers!"

Barbaros gives the standard "Alaikum-Salaam, welcome to Kaffir Buerger, where the falafel is a mouthful and the figs taste like pig."

I didn't get it. Did we even sell figs? I turned to the customer, giving what would be my final eulogy, "Salami Legume!"

Both men turned to me suspiciously, as if the accidental perversion of the greeting meant I was a saboteur on the inside. I was dismissed early by Barbie, who was so affected by the deviation/addition of the greeting as a prefix for a bean joke that he told me to go home without making eye contact—staring out of the Kaffir Buerger's mirrored windows, holding back his Turkish tears.

"Are you sure you don't need any shish impaled?"

"Just go," he said, imagining himself pumping gas into an Aston Martin somewhere near the Bosphorus.

I dreamed from a sleeping bag that night: an epic battle between the forces of lentil good and lima bean evil. The two beans battled to be the leaders of the Legume civilization. The Limasian government had convinced its people that Lentilians were not civilized, going so far as to accuse the Lentil government of conspiring with the Soyists. In the end, a battle between Lima and Lentil raged until all that was left was an odd porridge, which lacked any real depth or taste. Cue Onioninians.

Love Curse Number 1

"Ya know, in certain countries they tear your balls off for staring."

Olivia's first words to me came the day of my performance of "Love Curse" at the Abandoned Church. "Curse," for short, is a three minute epic ballad I wrote inspired by a bat trapped in a coffee filter who consequently turns to a sponge for the hot water boiling his tiny bat brain. The show was just me playing guitar and singing the song, like I had done previously for the Homeless Boys & Girls Club of Far Rockaway. The judge was a Filipino drag queen, Bino Del Griggio, or to those in the know, Miss Lolo Holo. Lolo belonged to a core group of elite judges, who insisted on being referred to as the Subvert Illuminatus, at the Abandoned Church, founded on the principles of

Friends to the friendless, Hearts for the heartless, and Farts for the fartless. I discovered this troupe of wombats and renegade bohemians after being dropped off at a hospital by my then so-called mother. She claimed that due to pesky unforeseen circumstances, I was better off a ward of state. Those circumstances roughly equated with her second husband jumping off a bridge and her third marriage to a cousin from Dublin, all resulting from my Muslim biological father abandoning her on a gondola on their honeymoon in Venice. I was told that Mook-tar Kaan's last words were, "I forgot to water my olive tree."

Incidentally, I've always wanted to find the gondola in question and burn it in a bloody show of symbolic birth rage.

Miss Lolo Holo could care less for my origin myth. She cherished her black kohl eyeliner and other fags. I wasn't a fag or into mutual mastication, so my rehearsal had to consist of some kind of talent. It wasn't easy but I finally became a finalist in their Tour de Force Hack talent show. The prize? Keys to the attic studio for a month, where the chosen artist could live and perfect their art. My talent—doing a sing-song with my busted Fender Stratocaster. After many attempts at memorizing my own lyrics (to no avail), I decided I would cheat and read the lyrics while playing. The years of hard livin' had caught up with my feeble memory and remembering lyrics I had written was nearly impossible.

There I sat on the night of show, waiting for Brunelle's Amazing Dog Toss to be over, wondering where I would be sleeping afterwards.

"I wasn't even looking at you," I said to the girl I would later deflower in a stolen police mini-car.

"Yes you were. You were staring, and your balls should be chopped off for it."

"Look, people only stare in bad short stories. I was admiring your elvish good looks. Jesus."

Brunelle tossed her dog through a ring of hula-hoop fire—she missed. The dog wheezed.

"I've heard that line before. Is that all you third-world hipsters think about? Tolkien's imaginary ideal of womanhood."

I reply, "You really should say what's on your mind, it might help you."

"And what's that, mister fortuneteller?"

The fire burned most of the little dog's hair clean off. Brunelle, struggling for a sparse applause, thanked the audience of miscreants for coming and dragged her convulsing poodle away. Lolo took the stage.

I told the girl next to me, "I'm about to go on. Just listen to the song, it might clue you in." She rolled her eyes, as if anything I could do or say would pull my swarthy impression out of her.

"And now we have something so banal for you, it might border on purposeless trash. Asking this kid where he's from is like asking Estelle Getty for your perm back."

A beer bottle flies across the stage smashing on the wall. A distant laugh is quelled by a sharp smacking sound. "He claims he's American, but this son-of-a-bitch is on a one way course to identity crisis city. Punks and Queens, I introduce Jeeeehad 'Do NOT call him Arab' McBaconface."

I walk onto the stage to a cacophony of booing and bored sighs, swooping my guitar strap to the front, and my mouth slams into the microphone making a loud bump sound out of the sound system.

"For fuck's sake!" Someone yells from the audience.

"This is my first time performing for an audience…"

I squint to try to make out who my audience is. They include: Miss Lolo Holo and her stocky white, bald financier; Olivia and her South Brooklyn entourage; Xris, her skinhead brother who watches from the makeshift bar; Mr. Ballacous, the Greek caretaker of the church who watches from behind the stage; the Far Rockaway Crusties, a crew of around ten nihilist punk rockers; and a smattering of the Coney Island Everquest Goths, particularly Jonas and Chiara.

Jonas, a Kurt Cobain look-a-like post-shotgun-to-the-skull shouts, "His name is Jehan not Jihad!"

"Thanks for the support, everyone. Since we're burning dogs tonight, this song is about a boiled bat. It's called Love Curse." I dug into my back pocket for the crumbled lyric sheet. "I have a terrible memory," I admitted. "Can't seem to remember my own songs."

I uncrumpled the paper, reviewing my lyrics while giving half-smiles to the crowd so as to keep their precious and smelly attention. They were feigning interest. A red haired orphan girl shouted loudly, "It's a hard knock life…"

cueing the rest of the audience to reply in unison, "FOR US!!"

I hit the mostly out of tune first notes and begin singing like the ghost of 1922 lounge singer.

Now you-ooo-ooo went away,
you left me heeeee-re to stay…

The song was rhythmically a dirge, like Billy Holiday singing at her own funeral mourning her lack of penetration into the Asian market, while simultaneously wishing for unmanned space flight.

And in the end you took it all,
left me here to take the fall,
Now you and I had it bad,
it was the worst time I ever had
Lord, I know it could be worse,
in this blue fluorescent time—Love is a curse!"

As I strummed the last notes, Miss Lolo Holo was grabbing the microphone from in front of my face.

"Where exactly was the bat in a coffee filter?" She asked cynically from stage left.

"It was inspired by the vision of one… I guess?" I responded, swooshing my guitar back behind me.

Perplexed by my response, Miss Lolo storms onto the stage and reclaims the mic. "Why do you write songs, Jihad?"

Usually a performer gets some kind of applause. The Abandoned Church was a tough love thing.

Jonas yelled again, "His name is Jehan not Jihad!"

"I can do other things. I just thought what I sung about needed to be sung, not written or illustrated."

Miss Lolo turned to the finalists, patiently waiting their turn on stage. "You see kiddies, here's a picture perfect example of a lost boy who needs to write a memoir and throw his guitar into the Hudson." She leaned into me and whispered, "And try not to use the retrospective retelling first person to tell your memoir—no one wants to read more ethnic melancholia from pudding bay."

"Wow," I get up swinging my guitar back behind me, "so much for self-referential torture music."

"Up your game and lose the dog collar. It accentuates your overall doggishness." She waves my breath odor away from the microphone whilst adjusting her Farah Fawcett wig. "Whew! Any more final words from halitosis boy?"

I begin to walk off stage, mumbling, "I'm not wearing a dog collar."

"Yeah, well that comment was inspired by the vision of you wearing one."

"Next time I'll do my nude performance art piece, 'When We Were Ravers.' Perhaps old techno and glowstick love would keep your attention longer." I snapped back.

"And he's snarky." Miss Lolo gave me a wink as I walked back to my seat. She gave another pointed introduction for the next act, a shrieking cellist, referring to her as "having the voice of a half-eaten lioness."

I put my guitar back in its case and sat down, turning to Olivia, who until then was simply the ornery girl from earlier (as opposed to being the ornery girl from South Essex, which would imply British influence of which I plead the fifth), "So what country exactly would tear my nuts off for looking at you?"

At around that moment I would meet her brother, Xris, who grabbed my shoulder and remarked from a place of beat down authority, "I used to be a skinhead."

He gulped his last drops from a can of one-dollar Pap Smear Ribbon. "Was it the Minor Threat skins or the KKK kind?" I asked, the former being a punk band that railed against any sick ideology the latter proposed. Xris, your untypical hardcore kid, took himself back to his early days as a career gutter punk racist, an overt one. Nowadays, the only difference is he's inert and politically correct, which means everything is everything and nothing is nothing.

"Man, I don't care about that race shit! Plus you don't even know what your'e fuckin' talkin' about." He released my shoulder as I soothed it.

Olivia told her brother, "You're the cleaner Xris, go polish off some more beer please."

"So what do you think I am?" I continued from a snail's perspective. I could have been dressed in full Sultan-wear decorated with a bright blue turban, brandishing a crescent sword and badly groomed handlebar mustache.

Of course, I would be shrunken and stuffed in a jar tapping the glass for more *mantu*.

"You some kind of ethno-punk wannabe I'm guessing. Quit that shit. Punk is punk, you don't have to pretext it with your race culture identity crap."

"Hey, you and your brother said I was, I never said anything about…"

Xris drifts away to the shoddily crafted bar, a pickle barrel containing cheap beer protected by some questionably dark skinned brother named Jaffar Heroin (whose left arm was entirely covered with rubber bracelets, tattoos and slithers of chainmail).

"Did my song suck that bad?" I asked her grinning. "It's a tough crowd," she grinned back.

On stage, the Tantamonious Red Baron of Canarsie Park bowed to bleak applause. Had I paid attention, I'm sure his history of the tulip crisis of 1634 told through animal voices would have astonished me. Ms. Lolo took to the stage again, now dressed in a Wonder Woman costume.

"Without further adieu, tonight's winner is the new guy." She held up a set of keys. "That's you, ethno-punk, now get up here."

Bacon comes alive!

Before momma donated her son to the sanitarium for state guidance and before I began living in an attic under the tutelage of a transgendered atheist alien named Lolo, Alistair Crowley and his Church of the Flesh was the closest I ever came to organized religion. I was more of a tarotist then a terrorist. I would pull all-nighters with Happy Jerry, my token reformed Jewish friend (no *yarmulka* on Passover), reading Wiccan spells from *The Necronomicon* for weather changes, money, and fortune, in that order. Oddly enough, some of our spells worked. Once we made it snow, or so I thought, which made it a no school day. Though we never actually performed the spell, I would insist the school closing was a matter of something we had done months earlier. Jerry would agree and usually leak our supreme abilities to classmates.

"Jerry, remember that money spell we did over the summer?" A teenaged version of me said.

"Not really." Jerry said in his pubescent cracking voice.

"You know the one where we read all of Lucifer's demon buddies in order—"

"Oh right, and I couldn't pronounce the last phrase."

He actually pronounced English words incorrectly. Jerry referred to milk as "melk" until he got married to a linguist at the ripe old age of 32.

"Well anyway, if we got huge sums of money from the sky, we could buy jet-packs. It's gonna happen—you gotta believe me, Jerr."

He nodded with feigned disinterest. I felt like a twenty-first century cyber shaman in training on a Brooklyn roof.

The idea was to use witchcraft to avoid school and take off into a Pinocchio candy land. We would stand on Brooklyn rooftops yelling phrases in Latin (ripped from the pages of over-the-counter pharmacy spell books), tricking ourselves into believing the demon conjurations were real.

"Jerry, did you feel that?"

Happy Jerry stared dispassionately into my eyes. "No. What happened?"

"I felt a breeze! It worked!"

If a cold wind blew or a car drove by, we would take that as a sign of having satisfied one of many demons we had learned from *Dungeons & Dragons Advanced Compendium Volume II*. Small events became extraordinary. Just healthy pre-teen rebellion and heavy metal–induced Satanism—no big deal. As I got older and realized the "do what thou wilt" philosophy at the core of Satanism suited a wealthier person than myself (someone who could afford the luxury of free orgies in Italy with the mandatory Vatican-sponsored after party exorcisms), I switched gears and discovered Erich Von Daniken's *The Chariots of the Gods*, which put forth the idea that God was an ancient astronaut. The proof was in the hieroglyphs and "abandoned airfields" of several extinct civilizations.

Upon discovering this concept I drew back my early nineties ponytail (the sides of the head shaved though, to distinguish from the last generation of ponytailers). "We're alien-human hybrids!" I thought, "I knew it all along."

My alien powers ceased to make inanimate objects move or glow. If I was half alien, why did my meditations on metallic water not yield any forgotten formulas? Either I had superpowers, or there was a conspiracy. Enter Robert Anton Wilson, stage right, with his *Illumunatus!* trilogy telling me it was all a paranoid game by the old America connected through secret societies all the way to, yup you guessed it, pre-Islamic Iran. RAW. as he is known, was probably the closest guru I had until Ram Das, or was it the other way around? It surely wasn't Ronald Reagan or the Ayatollah for that matter. Mayan hieroglyphics and the eye inside the pyramid of the holy dollar bill was the only proof I needed of a higher force. These ancient relics and symbology implied that if there was contact with extraterrestrials, it must have been by a secret society that now runs the show. Aliens, disguised as humans (probably working in the secret service) not Satan, were now the great creators of my universe until Carlos evicted the whole bunch. Oh, Carlos Castaneda, that crazy anthropologist, he threw me for a deep swell. Forget the men in black and white warlocks, Carlos pointed to the secret being in Mexico. The great Nagual master Don Juan told Carlos to seek the truth not through prayer, incantations, or in the sky but inter-dimensionality. They're called the Allies, and they roam our world taking on forms like faceless hitchhikers and giant squirting Mexican Shamans (i.e., Don Juan himself [*squirt squirt*]). The trick was you had to partake in the great root in order to access this "mystical world." You had to dose on 'shrooms.

I pulled the second batch of frozen fake pork strips out of the fridges of Kaffir Beurger, my floppy pig hat nearly falling from my head. Barbaros was angry again. "Not enough customers!" he complained as he chased a few out with shish impalers for asking for tzatziki sauce.

"Can you put extra tzatziki sauce on that please?" They would ask. "No!" He would shout, "That is a Greek thing, we are Turkish!"

Follow that up with a furrowed stare down contest between customer and owner; end with a climactic chase scene; imagine *Cannonball Run* meets

Green Card.

Having won the talent show and now having a modicum of stability, a place to rest my head, today was a rather good day. I appreciated Barbaros. Before the dude gave me this job, most of my time was spent in a narcotic-induced creative hysteria, dropping hit after hit of acid, thinking the doors of fame perception would open. If Jim Morrison's path had any logic to it, all I had to do was trip out at the beach and play guitar until the mighty rock'n'roll gods gave me the secret talisman to stardom. Seems like a good plan, until you need to get a job and grow up. Barbaros was questioning me on my career plans that moment.

"What are you doing, Jehan?" Barbaros asked. "You should be in school, not wandering all over the place."

The strips sizzled to a rhythm in my head making a sound akin to some early polyrhythmic Frank Zappa instrumental. The bacon came alive like Peter Frampton's breakthrough record in 1976, the year of my birth. The slices popped themselves up, the lead one (I knew he was the lead because of his glam-rock disco hair) holding what appeared to be a screeching v-neck guitar.

"Ladies and gentleman of the greater Rockaway area," he shouted. "I am Mr. Riddlin' Hog and we are HOGZILLA. This is the first song off our new album *Bacon Comes Alive.*" The Italian drummer, Señor Salvatore yells, "And not the Kevin one! Hit it!"

The grease boiled on the grill thick along with the irony, Hogzilla's first record was called *Six Degrees to Fakin' Bacon.* "What a bunch of crazy slabs," I thought.

Señor Salvatore, the drumming strip o' phony bacon, banged out a beat on his little drum kit as Riddlin' railed out a screeching guitar riff. Emerging from the top right of the grill, a strip of bacon wearing cool sunglasses pounded on his thick bass guitar. My jaw dropped, as did the floundering rubber hog on my head.

"Pick your hat up, Jehan, look presentable. Customers are coming in." Barbaros was unaware of the slithering slab's impromptu performance on his grill.

"This is amazing," I thought, readjusting the rubber cap. Riddlin' started singing to the heaviest instrumental ever:

Liberation!
Emancipation!
We here to start the show!
All you mother-frickers about to glow!

So don't take it light.
Get your guns and – Fa, fa, fa – FIGHT!

Fa, fa, fa – fafafa, FALAFEL!
Da, da, da – dadada, Delightful!
Can't get enuff of that tzatziki stuff
Everybody in the house, let tear this up!

"Stop, stop stop," I said to the grilling band. "It's white sauce, not tzatziki. That's Greek. You're in a Turkish joint!"

Hogzilla stopped, Mr. Hog pissed off and in an acquired Scottish twang yelled, "Fer fucks sake, Jehan, it's a freekan'g song. A moos'ical poem!"

Barbaros looked at me suspiciously. I leaned in and whispered, "I know and it's great Mr. Hog, but if the boss hears the lyrics..."

"Fuck your boss, man! You shouldn't even be working here. Go to the studio and start laying some tunes down. It's your only hope. We're out." Riddlin' turned to his band, said something in Pig Latin, and they turned back into lifeless broils.

It was around that time that she walked in with her dad, a very formal guy dressed in black wearing the Jewish skullcap, a *yarmulka*. I took one look at her dirty *Payless* bunny snow princess boots and knew these two had differences. A puffy light blue jacket with pink sweatpants covered her up, but my super-Sufi x-ray eyes caught the curve around the buttock area. Suddenly, I was disinterested in my career path and heard Rumi love sonnets.

"I won the talent show and I'm gonna be a rock star, Barbaros. You'll see, then I'll buy this place and franchise it across the globe."

He let out a deep Mediterranean laugh while talking to the customers. "Right, you keep on dreaming, Jehan."

I gave the daughter a quick smirk, her eyes catching me in the act of unholy observation.

"Welcome to Kaffir Beurger! Where the pigs are figs and the Gyro is holy!" Barbaros exclaimed with his usual vague pomposity.

Her dad took one look at me as I flipped the phony bacon to the side, asking Barbaros, "Is everything on the menu kosher?"

"Kosher?" Barabaros' inner thought–adjuster juxtaposed the idea of kosher with idea of halal. "Yes, it's halal, blessed by the holiest clerics on the west side of the East Coast." The man's daughter giggled slightly as her dad pondered the great rift between halal and kosher. Again, I engaged in a deeper mental undressing of her as our eyes met like a quasar slamming into a black hole of intercultural boom.

"I admire your strict adherence to divine preparation," said the father, exhibiting a deeper knowledge probably gained in his yeshiva years. "We are Jewish and only eat divinely blessed food."

"You've come to the right place, my Jewish friend. Here at Kaffir Beurger we are all two-dimensional characters whittled down to our race and religion—or the children of Abraham." Barbie opened his arms.

"Children of Abraham in da house!" I yelled, putting up one arm and waving it like, *I just don't care.*

The new customer, who took it upon himself to identify himself as Jewish eight times within sixty seconds, was now convinced that Abraham's children were in the house (actually Mook-tar's children, and who knew how many eyebrows Barbie's dad had). "I've decided," he said. "We're in a rush, so we will try the special Kaffir burger and a side of hummus."

"Will that be to stay or to go?" asked Barbie.

He conferred with his daughter for a moment as I hummed the chorus to the Clash's song of the same title, while slicing a pepper anticipating them to order the special.

"Darlin' you got to let me kno-oooow,
Oh whoa whoa—should I stay or should I…"

"Is this good for you?" he tenderly asked his daughter, like the rub of an undercooked tenderloin.

She ignored him, as if his tenderness was a social mask for the growth hormones that lay deep in the tenderoni boneys. Instead, hearing my im-promptu quiet tribute she hummed back, "If I stay there will be trouble."

His voice turned into an overcooked rib-cut, terse, quick, demanding. "Dalya! I asked a question!"

Picking up her last line and seeing his growing impatience, I flipped a chunk of meat on the grill and sang, "If I go, there will be double."

She was a different creature entirely, bearing zero resemblance to the old man, and gentler—kind of like Ronald Reagan's brief South Bronx visit. She was a dark skinned pimento, and he was just a hard, unsoaked white legume.

"Ok, we'll have to take the order to go, please," he told Barbaros, who then commanded me to get back to work. Her dad reminded her, "Dalya, get your head out of the clouds, you are about to meet your future husband, my future son-in-law!"

"Not if I can help it," she smirked. Oh, how the smirk is contagious.

I tossed together their order and slipped the hottie my cell number on a napkin. She slyly took a look at it:

Jehan (happy face) You're my new muse, use this for a free Nutshake. Come again. (picture of pig with a kufi)

Before her dad could see, she nodded at me with a soft excitement, and the two took off.

Mr. Riddlin' Hog, now part of a larger conglomeration of other hog strips, came back to life one more time and gave me a solid little wink out of his cartoon eyes. He then pillaged though onion and pepper bits to pull his bandmates out of the pile. "Hogzilla, you in there!" he called.

"Jehan!" Barbie yelled, my floppy pig hat jumping from the echo.

"Jeez, what's up?"

"No singing while customers are here. It looks bad." Barbie burped.

"No singing? C'mon, there's no rule that says—"

"Look," his mono-brow dominant, "I run the holiest burger shop in Rockaway. It is against our *tawhid* to sing in a place of worship."

He had obviously missed the boat on the thousands of years of ritual chanting and dancing in Sufi Islam.

"Ever since you won that damned contest, you think you're some kind of rock star." The unfortunate old Turk grabbed the knife from my hand. "If you want to continue working here, no singing."

I just took it in, slightly dazed and confused. The Slithering Slabs got re-united and banged out the last words of the song:

Should I stay or should I go!

Beach Daze

The summer was in full swing. The Ramones' "Rockaway Beach" blared out of every rehab bar from Beach 116th Street down to the boardwalk. Armies of drunk widows kicked their dying and/or passed out scarecrow counter-parts. Days passed as I chased inspiration in the Rockaway waves to no avail, occasionally taking some time to hang with the bizarre kids around me. I would kill time up in the attic arranging a slew of inspirations into incomplete song recordings that went nowhere. Nothing was coming out. I was a wilted jellybean with no core, or a jellybean flower wilting with no jelly. I had a ripped-up sofa to sleep on, a busted guitar to play on, and a buggy computer with ridiculously hard software to record with. Technically, any would-be rockstar genius would be able to make lemonade out of these lemons. I began doubting I could follow up "Love Curse" with anything else.

"Fuck! I can't even play this guitar," the lower E popped off the neck after a frustrating strum.

There was something I had the responsibility to create, and it wasn't streaming into my head—like a dangerous gas leak in a welfare apartment, I was losing steam with 9/11 miles away.

Ms. Lolo Holo opened the crumbling wooden door. Her wardrobe com-bination scared me: a pink summer miniskirt with yellow taffeta wrapped around her stringy neck, white sunglasses covering the Filipino boy eyes, and fake boobs intact.

"What's today's date, Gee?" she asked, pecking towards the computer. I was a shirtless savage, my hair down; perched on a stool about to destroy the guitar from the last failed notes.

"Dude, I lost my track of time in '93 after a bad trip. Isn't it Saturday?" I asked.

"Right, too much information, Jihad. And I'm a dudette, in case you didn't notice," she replied over-caffeinated. "Okay, okay." She checked the date on the lower right of the monitor. "It's August 28th, 2001. Time to upgrade your time clock, Gee."

I laughed. "Seems like '93 was the last year the world mattered anyway. Did the computer get that last take?"

"Don't ask me. And quit the victimhood—remember, your readers hate brown self-pity. I don't know how to use this machine. If you're talking about that window thing that was just open that said recording, I shut it off."

"Oh fabulous, Lolo." This drag queen was becoming a drag. I retired the old Stratocaster to its stand and stretched out, looking through the triangular attic window.

"By the way, Jihad," she said like an office clerk about to ask for their daily reports, "Kurt kicked the can in '94, so add a year to your definition of the end of time. And stop looking out the window like that—put a bunch of rags on your head and a teardrop, and you're the sad Arab again."

Wow, I thought, that would mean it's been over five years since Nirvano took the "More than a Feeling" riff and mutilated it into "Smells like Reems Spirit." Where do the days go? The horror.

"I'm not pilfering memories, Lolo, it's just damn hot today and the gods of rockstardom are all tanning." Beads of sweat dripped down my forehead as I watched Raymond put Jaffar in a headlock in the church courtyard. "I got nothing, Lolo, I'm an empty vessel." Yancy stole two handfuls of beer as Raymond kept Jaffar in the headlock.

"That's pretty obvious, and you need to take a shower. You smell like fried chickpeas." Lolo scuffled a stack of bad paintings of herself silkscreened in neon colors from one side of the attic to the other.

"That's from the restaurant. My natural odor is less ethnic."

"I'm sure. Well listen, kiddo, you got another couple of days to use the space. If you're not feeling the creative juices flowing out of your little brain, try out at the next talent show, and maybe you can get another month."

"Are you guaranteeing that I'll win?" I asked sarcastically.

Lolo came over to me and squeezed my face with one very veined masculine hand. It felt strange. There was makeup on her knuckles. "You're cute, Jihad, but not that cute. Now go find some inspiration. I have a date with the gas station guy. He said I had beautiful boobs."

Oh man, what a disgusting thing to imagine, but she was my temporary landlord. "I thought your boobs were—" Lolo moved from squeezing my face to covering my mouth.

"Don't say it! Nothing's fake around here except the new guy who doesn't socialize and spends all his time in the attic, right—poser?"

"Mmmm," I mumbled through covered lips as she uncovered them and began walking out. "And the bacon."

"What?"

"The bacon… that's also fake," I said.

Lolo sighed. "Punch lines without punch, that should be the name of your album!" She shut the broken wooden door and took off, the sound of unfitting high heels clacking down the staircase. I threw on one of two shirts I owned, an old t-shirt with a logo of a frog spitting its tongue out and eating a little girl, probably the logo for some defunct rave or skate company.

I ran down the spiraling staircase of creaking termite-ridden boards and out into the church courtyard. A broken cross, probably once inside the building (which really wasn't a building anymore, considering most of the outer walls were destroyed years ago), now stood up by sheer luck against a corner. Xris sat next to it and called me over.

"Yo!" he shouted, his voice shooting through the world's worst death punk volleyball match going on between us.

"Yo!" I shouted back, walking over to him. He spit next to my foot like a Roman soldier claiming Western China. "You makin' some good art upstairs or what?"

"Tryin' to, buddy," I replied, rubbing his spit around with my Converse. Little did he know the Roman brigades would fall for the goji berries creating generations of little Gushi blue-eyed Asian pot-smokers. "Must be the right time, right place."

"Ya know, I had that space last month," he interrupts. Jonas gets smacked on the head with the volleyball and jumps on Keon, the Rasta-punk opponent that spiked him. Jonas was the Kurt Cobain look-a-like who belonged to the Coney Island Everquest Goths. Recently, he decided to start dreadlocking his shoulder length blonde hair for all the wrong reasons. His over-application of beeswax mixed with complete incompetence of why a Rastafarian dreads their hair silently offended most of the punk rock brothers in the church.

"What was your talent?" I asked, expecting "crushing watermelons with my buttocks" to be the answer.

"My dad's talent. He's a public speaker and ex-journalist." His tone revealed that he didn't think much of his own abilities. "Dad won the damn contest, and they gave him the studio, but he never used it, so I just crashed there." Xris scratched specks of dirt off the cross. "He's gonna do his thing again at the next competition, so you might have a match up ahead of you."

"You call the talent show a competition? That was more like a guide to burning poodles and a Rockaway wombat singing 'Danny Boy.'" I maneuvered away from Jonas, who flew by me, thrown by Keon, dreads flying. "Anywho, a musician versus a journalist sounds interesting," I end.

As stated earlier, violence was a turn off—made me cringe. Jonas hit the ground hard, his 110 pound heroin body wrenching and moaning on the ground as his sticky adhesive fake locks attached the dirt to him like a magnet. His opponent mounted him, preparing to cross hook punch.

"The I a look fi' trouble youth! I n I fight fire youth man," Keon balked, releasing a wail of pent up frustration with Jonas' choice of hair.

Xris grabbed a beer bottle from the floor, cracking it on the cross to make the shard ends a skin shredder. "Dude, please don't do that," I asked Xris. The sound alerted the fiasco that things were just about to get bloody. He ignored me and walked towards the two erratics. "Yo," he yelled. Thinking twice about surgery from a sliced spine, Keon retracted. Xris gripped the bottle shard with a newfound sense of purpose. "Okay, man, okay. It's just a game, no hurt no problem," Keon turned to Xris, the baldhead enforcer. Jonas crawled out from under the grapple.

"No problem for you or no problem for me?" Xris asked, wrapping Keon's dreadlocks in his fist and pulling him up and away.

"Tonight's beer on I Xris," Keon said, expecting I wouldn't see his smirk to the other Rasta-punks who watched on the side. Meanwhile, Xris stood, the lone warrior, ready to take the upper hand in any violence that might happen. It just didn't look like a swell ending to a stupid moment, so I backed off, not wanting to be associated with Xris on the debate. I escaped the volleyball game with the busted net, in the busted courtyard, in the busted church with the busted drama. Anything was better than the smell of acrid alcohol and huddles of punky rock orphans.

Welcome to Rockaway Beach! A world of beach homes and wombats with straw hats, high or drunk from sucking Guinness taps where a patch of fake green grass, a.k.a. Astroturf, was on sale in front of the Ninety-Nine Cent store (where nothing was actually 99 cents at all). I push my hair back, taking in the Rockaway unglory. It made me question what I was doing in general.

"What are you doing in general?" I heard from behind me. "Huh?" I said, pirouetting like a shocked Mikhail Baryshnikov after a giant nut prop dropped on his partner in a performance of *Nutcracker*. It was Olivia, the girl from the church who threatened to tear off my nuts, eating what appeared to be a mango. She bit into the mango nut, cracking it. *Crack!*

"It's you," I said, the raw inspiration of my Astroturf amazement now fading away. She sucked up the bits of mango nut, licking the juices off her little Irish lips. "Haven't seen you in a while," she added as I turned down a secluded block.

"I'm not in the mood for your nihilistic persuasions, woman. Is your brother always so accommodating?" I asked.

"A way with words young Padawan has." She mimes a Yoda voice. "Xris? What, did he hang you off the ledge or something?" She giggled, tracking me from behind.

"Aren't we the giggly one, wanting to bite off my balls? I'm not really into the anarchist head bashing mentality around here. Doesn't inspire me much." Had she not popped up, I would have probably had an album inspired by fake grass. I eyed the police mini-mobile tucked in the corner of a lot.

"Not up to your standards?" she asked, looking at me. "Looking for glass towers and shiny dew drops on rose pedals or something?"

"Oh, that's clever. You don't even know me and there you go..."

Before my grumpy protest went on, Olivia jumped in front of me, stopping me in my tracks. The August heat blistered down on us through uninterrupted skies. She pushed my hair back, then gently grabbed the back of my neck with both hands and pulled herself up to eye level, whispering, "Listen, if you want inspiration, you need to have a little fun Rumpelstiltskin."

Then she landed it, a great wet American kiss destined for France. I stood totally still as if Medusa mesmerized Hercules. My lips relaxed on hers, twisting together setting off a planted network of atomic explosions from the Mumbai to Antarctica of my mind. All blossoming into mushrooms clouds filled with ideas—like a gang of Japanese kids flying penis-hover-bikes through rainy tunnels to escape the heat blast. Note to self: carry a pad around with you in case of spontaneous human female attacks. The Ramones played on:

> Rock, rock, rockaway beach,
> Rock, rock, rockaway beach,
> We can hitch a ride at Rockaway Beach.

Ethno-Punk

A note is taped on the doors of Kaffir Beurger:

> Jehan, open up shop *Anahtarlar paspasın altında*.
> And remember, no singing while working.

> Signed, B.

The Turkish part informed me the key was under the mailbox. My rudimentary grasp of modern Ottoman contained around twenty words—the rest was a guess. I never claimed fluency, just understanding enough to navigate through restaurant menus and carpet stores.

The last day of my free studio was looming over me like a cruel woman.

So much so that I didn't bother putting on the floppy rubber pig hat today. I opened the shop, prepared the shish and chicken kebobs, started the rice, crushed up the chickpeas, filled the fryer with oil, cut the veggies, then stood still behind the cash register channeling geniuses who dared sell millions of records with mollifying American love songs.

"Get on back jack," I hummed, "The straight and narrow ain't your path, so you want more." I wrote it down immediately. This first line was a sure-fire mainstream winner. A container of hot sauce next to me grabbed my attention. "But I'm sure the heat will cool and the sauce will…" It wasn't working. "Fuck, fuck, fuck," I mumbled, a thick nimbus of smoke emanating from the grill. I threw the half-doodle on a napkin out and turned off the grill. The front door blasted ajar. It was Keon and his deceptively benign Rasta-punk boys.

"Whaddagwan, Jehan!" He said, his boys going to the back and taking seats.

"Hey, what's going on, Keon." I knew for a fact these guys couldn't have any money to order anything with.

"Keon, Jee-on, we two flava's of the same cream youth. I is the dark cream and you is the—"

I interrupted him before he dared call me white. "Oh right, 'cuz our names rhyme. You want menus or anything?" I was beginning to sense a lethal tension in Keon's rectal region. He was coming off like a new brand of Jamaican drug pimp (filling in the missing niche for one in Rockaway). The problem with his acquired attitude was the law of substitution. You can't substitute a Rasta pimp with a weak little punk regardless of how many off-the-boat Caribbean stoners you add.

He flailed his arms as his crew nodded with violent agreement. "I ne' a been blut-clot, he push me down—ya'see I comes to warn you 'bout yo' de' baldhead bumbaclot."

"Uh-huh," I said. "Look, Keon, he ain't my boy. I don't know the kid. I'm just trying to make the music stuff happen."

Needless to say, if I was about to get a beating, at least they should know the backstory with me. "You too scared to hit Xris up straight. You come into my work like this? You don't even know me, kid."

Keon only heard the tone, not the content, and thus gave his best how-dare-you-cross-me shocked look. At this point, I took off my uniform top as his boys began moving towards me. I knew the deal. "I knew this was gonna happen," I said to myself, as if declaring it apocryphal would made the bruises heal easier.

"Blood clut, wot' u gonna do bumbaclo, come chru' on the outside…" he said, flipping his boys to pull me out as they walked out.

"Uh-huh, sure." I said, getting ready to take it, really just wanting to get back to writing. So many damn interruptions, I thought. They weren't going to get a fight out of me. I can talk my way out, run back in and close the door, I thought. Keon walked out ahead, his boys pushing me through the door, slapping me around and pronouncing curses in unintelligible Selaisse-I gibberish. They also blocked the door. Damn.

My final words, "You know I'm not white, right?" didn't do much to calm down the angry and stoned posse. "And I don't even know Xris that well."

"Don' come in mi face—ain' no' fault rasta.' I no care me I do 'dis buu-ullshit. You see I hand." He smacked me hard. "What color is 'dis?" I turned my head back to him, deciding not to answer his absurd interrogation. "Bang him out, bang him out—bop bop…" exclaimed one of his cronies, hands flailing. The general sense I got was these guys had worked themselves up for this. A hard fist from one of his scumbag crew entered my abdomen, and I keeled over.

"He ask you what color his hand is bredern," demanded the puncher.

I grumbled holding my aching stomach, "It's kind of… off-brown—you done?"

Keon took my head and began thrusting his knee into it. "Nah, we ain 'done whi' boy…" With the impact of the first kneeing to the head, I noticed his tattered old jeans and Birkenstocks on exposed dry feet—with highly ungroomed toenails.

"No Birkenstock wearing, Haile-Selaisse worshipping tree-hugger would get the pleasure of making me bleed," I thought. I just couldn't take the beating and pushed through the crew. Seeing as how I refuse to fight, Keon and his crew were grandstanding off of me.

"Clear the door gentleman, Jehan has work to do." It was Ms. Lolo Holo, floating down from the sky on a Hover-Poodle like a glam godsend, as the words *deus ex machina* flashed past us. We all stopped to admire her pink rubber dominatrix suit with accessory angel wings.

"A' mees' Lolo, we a just chreatin' the boy to a bit of 'dis bumbaclot Xris. 'Dat baldhead push me down, and we come for sum' vengeance an'ting."

"Listen boys," Lolo jiggled her fierce heroine self like a silverfish. "You have two options: get the fuck out of here and don't come back to the Church ever again, or get the fuck out of here, and don't come back to the Church again."

I rushed back inside. "Thanks, Lolo. Nice quaff, by the way." Keon's boys cleared the way, taking off in opposite directions (perhaps to claim the Jamaican pimp niche in other areas), ashamed that the great Filipino tranny caught them in mid-act.

"Why gracias, Señor Jihado," she said, fluffing her red wig and hitting the throttle on the flying poodle. "Tonight's the talent show and your time will be up in a few days. Chop-chop!"

"Don't remind me."

The audience was sparse that night. An odd tinge of apathy was in the air of those in attendance, and the acts were questionable. I scanned around at the few assorted characters, my attention span beginning to wane. A "normal" stood up and approached the stage. "Who's this guy?" I asked. Olivia had recently undergone a bad dye job, changing her hair from dirty blonde to pink-brown-yellow. Girls do the strangest things after getting de-virginized in a police mini-car.

"Oh god. You want to leave now. It's my dad."

"Your dad?" I choked.

Without warning the alpha dominant Ms. Lolo had her microphone yanked away. "Fuck," Olivia sunk into her hood, pink-brown-yellow strands of hair wrapping her face. "Irish eyes no longer smiling," I said as she winced. Her dad was way too hyped up for his own weight, wearing what amounted to a wardrobe from the Christian Dominionist's Corporate Slog-hound catalog of Broken Dreams and Injected Ideology, a white button down tucked into cheap slacks complete with pocket protector.

"We have an expression from my generation," he began. Lolo sneered.

"To quote Pink Floyd: The lunatic is in my head…"

Olivia got up from her chair abruptly, storming over to Jaffar Heroin at the beer barrel. I was confused.

"…However, here at this supposed nonprofit for a bunch of self-exoticized memes, the lunatics are outside my head."

"Shit," I thought. "Olivia's dad is a wee bit different from his daughter."

"You all gather here at Saint Mark's Church disrespecting and committing sacrilege towards the saints who came before you!"

"Enough, Malachy, your name's not on the list." The drag queen attempted to take the microphone back. Wonder Woman could not vanquish this automaton though.

"No! I don't need an invite from some faggot homosexual immigrant!" He yanked the mic back. The crowd began to wake up and a low frequency of boos began.

"First of all," Malachy continued to Lolo, now degenerated to his/her real face, simple Bino from the Philippines—or a sandcastle destroyed by a tidal wave. No quick-witted reaction, no wall of fire. Just Malachy owning the stage: "First of all!"

Lolo sank into the curtains, disappearing. The abuse would continue. He ranted about all the things wrong with the world (at that time): the gays, the immigrants, the liberals, and vegetarians. "And the kids! Look at you— dirty nods stuffed in your faces!"

"Huh?" I wondered. Jonas came over to sit next to me, his bad dreadlocks having been the adhesive to every known piece of matter on the eastern seafront. "Dude, I thought this was a talent show."

"Yeah, well, this is his talent," I said, deciding to let him in on my earlier experience. "You know, Keon threw me around today because of that bullshit with you the other day."

"Sorry about that—I heard. What a fuck wad," he replied, twiddling a single sad dreadlock.

"Jonas, quit the dreadlock look. It's not you at all," I demanded.

"I was thinking the same thing. Too hard to manage," he said, trying to unstick what appeared to be a chicken's whole foot from the tangle.

Olivia, at wit's end, huffed and puffed, chugged her can of *Pap Smear*

Ribbon, and stormed the stage shaking off her hood. "Dad, get off the stage!"

"My daughter," Malachy positioned himself, beads of sweat coming through a shirt way too small for his fubsy pudding of a body. "My quote unquote," facetiously fingering the quotes, "daughter. You're just mad because your mother left you."

Ripe for any potential physical squabble, Xris leapt from stage right, falling upon his own father in a fury, dragging him off the stage. "Olivia told you get off the stage, Dad, now get off the damn…"

She stood still, a mixture of humiliation and sadness biting her last words and stuck on the next ones. I placed my guitar against the loose crucifix to wipe the fresh tears from her face. "Mothers are just vessels to be discarded, don't pay him any attention," I advise her.

Malachy was making a ruckus as his son manhandled him like a prison warden. Now red in the face from his showcase of conservative rage, Malachy's dishonored fattened gaze landed on me.

"Au revoir, bean bag!" I yelled. The only possession I had fell from where it leaned. The Fender Stratocaster keeled over, its strings snapping off as the neck broke in two. Malachy began to laugh. "Disqualified! I win!" The cracked guitar, with its exposed innards, wood shards, and bouncing strings glazed me over.

"Oh no, Jehan, your guitar!" Olivia said under duress, her affection filtered through a feeling of partial responsibility for her father's stage rage.

Why was he laughing at me? I look like everyone here. Hamburger and french fries kids, outcasts yes, but all-American outcasts. The boos of the drunk punks drown out the cackling conservative, who vanishes into the dark, dragged off by his son. Ms. Lolo leaps onstage, now in full Wonder Woman attire, giving the newly activated crowd, apathetic, an accented interpretive performance of Episode 3, Season 1 of the show. She flounders across the stage with over-the-top distractions, ending with a cold and silent stare down to each and every one of us.

"No one wins and no one loses, people, now go home!" Lolo throws the mic down with belligerent malaise.

No fancy outros, no more guitar, and no keys to the studio—but that was tomorrow. I still had the night.

Lost Cause

I cleared the studio of the items I had accumulated there: old hummus containers, a handheld television I found, paper scribbles worth about two cents, and a slap in the face. Jaffar fiddled with the 1972 black and white television with a lobotomized cheerfulness. He reminded me of a second grader in the body of a dying junkie. Jonas was trying to make sense of the month of poor recordings I made, his skinny neck and sticky dreads hunched into the computer monitor.

"Did you record anything this month?" he asked. I stuffed a bag with my clothes and survival pack.

"Uh-huh. There should be something there, keep looking," I said, passing the attic window. There in the courtyard down below were Olivia and Keon. I guessed he had resurfaced after everyone left. Why is he talking with Olivia? I wondered.

"That Rasta is back," I said, low enough that the two J's didn't bother to acknowledge me. The television played images without sound. President and King–elect George working on his golf swing as text scrolled below the image that his approval ratings were at an all time low. I was sure there must have been more important things going on in the world. "Change this shit, Jaffar. I can't stand this guy."

"I can't believe you get any reception from this thing," he said in an inscrutable Arabic accent. He clicked around, settling on a UHF channel that only showed NASA footage. Today's episode was one shot of the earth from the International Space Station.

"Big planet," I remarked, starting to get tired. Jonas was deep in his headphones, passing a bag of mushrooms to Jaffar, who quickly palmed some into his mouth, his left arm bandaged with rubber bracelets and accessories that jingled as he lifted the 'shroom.

"Why you got so much shit on your left arm?" Jonas yelled from inside his headphones.

I reached over and pulled one side of the headphone off so he could hear me. "Dude, you don't have to yell that loud." A fan the size of an apple hung near the back of the computer, the Church's low-budget air conditioner and provider of white noise.

"So my left arm won't get jealous of my right," Jaffar said, switching channels with his right hand. He tossed me the remainder of the bag of 'shrooms. Chunks of dried stems and caps, the poor man's medication for the reality blues, emptied into my mouth.

"This tastes like a cat's ass. Where's the water?" I said.

"It's grown on shit, that's the point!" Jaffar replied.

"What's the point of the point though? I just lost my opportunity to become the world's next twentysomething pop savior." I released a victimized sigh and plopped down on the sofa I would no longer be sleeping on.

Jonas lifted one side of his headphones. "August 11th to September 11th ain't a long time to produce a masterpiece album. At least you got a job at the burger joint. Look at the bright side." Jonas dredged through the computer, looking for anything. I knew there was nothing to find except short takes of guitar riffs, the main idea for "Get on back Jack," and maybe a catchy chorus or two. No real songs, no real lyrics.

"Plus," mentioned Jaffar, "look at us. You and I are not the kind of kids that become famous."

His comparison didn't strike a chord in me. "The Bee Gees finished the whole *Saturday Night Fever* record in a weekend. No excuse. You can write a hit song off any dumb idea."

His mouse clicks were the answer. There was nothing to find. "Hold on a second, I think I found something." He clicked and the opening notes to "Jack" played. "Oh, this is good." Then it stopped. "Damn, that was short. Is that all you got recorded?"

Through the window, I continued to watch Olivia, who appeared angry at first, but was now warming up to Keon. What a whore! I thought, sliding over to the sofa. Gets laid for the first time in her life and turns into insta-slut.

"The whole celebrity rock star myth rides off the idea of Satanic-induced chaos—again jerk offs jerking off," I offered as a philosophical excuse to my laziness. "You end up sounding like a Fred Lurst wannabe mixing every genre that makes money." I licked the bits of hallucinogenic mushrooms caps from my teeth.

Jaffar ended the debate. "Yeah, but he's a wannabe, so you wannabe a wannabe—cancels you out. You become a useless twit who gets to buy big houses and sleep with plastic people, but you live far away from real human beings and become an alien scientologist."

Jerk offs. Musicians were all jerk offs—spoiled poets. Rockers were scumbags and the rappers were egoists, at least that was the going notion in my head. Writers, now there's something I might want to look into. Maybe I was too nice. Maybe I need to rob some old ladies, beat up a few Hare Krishnas.

"Useless twit, huh? Who said I'm against turning into an alien?" I reacted. Jaffar switched the channel again.

Better Off Dead was on, the tale of a useless suicidal twit. "Oh, leave this scene on," Jonas screeched. "It's the car race with the chinks." Jonas turned back to his software bliss and the 'shrooms started to kick in. My voice slurred, words sounding strange as I said them: "Donnnnn't caaa…lll Chinese people chi…nks."

"You already are an alien, Jehan," Jaffar said in a voice akin to Vincent Price introducing *Swamp Thing*. He lifted his arm of bracelets and rubber bands, sounding off the jingle-jangles, his body vibrating in succession with the sounds in the room. Within the span of three seconds and one sentence, I entered the land of the great root.

"Yeah, dude, like, what are you?" Jonas said as I lay on the sofa, sinking deeper into it. I looked at him hunched over the computer, then at Jaffar, who seemed to be moving in circles. Unable to close my eyes, the image on the television no longer fit into the square center of its device shell, instead growing exponentially like a blanket being stitched over you. John Cusack's character in the movie became an unwilling opponent to a drag race. As the image grows over me the characters become us. I am the unwilling opponent in some drag race. My head transfixed to the drool stained pillow.

"I'm tripping hard!"

The Freaks Come Out at Night

"Lay'deez and Gentle'man! Big Up Flatbush!" Keon says through a megaphone in the voice of what Howard Cossell would sound like if he went through the Brumblefly machine with Bob Marley. Also driving is Xris, both men dressed in brown tweed leisure suits.

I drive up in a puttering station wagon pulling to a stop at the red light. "Shit, not these guys again."

"We have here a fight to the finish, a virtual battle for American rock stardom the likes of which has never been seen."

"Look guys, I really don't think this is—"

"On one side, Jehan 'Don't call me Arab' McBacon-face…"

In vain, I shout over the megaphone, "Not my name, Keon. I'm not doing this!"

"…and on the other side, the great white hope, Xris Kristopherson Krodawg, back from his last championship race versus the Russian-Asian Sensation, Chow Young Blatt, who suffered a mighty defeat and was deported back to Bahausistan."

Xris slowly turns his head to me, revealing an army knife gripped down in his teeth. He growls.

"Now Xris," I say, trying to calm the beast, "I didn't sign up for this."

His final words to me before the light turns green: "DRIVE ETHNO-PUNK!"

I attempt to put the car in gear fast enough, nervously slamming on the gas. Xris and Keon zoom ahead, leaving a huge plume of smoke in their trails. I go shooting in reverse, front-ending the car behind me. The logo of an overexcited pig wearing a kufi decorates the smashed car's door. Barbaros, a bit fatter and more unshaven than usual, brutally ejects himself from his destroyed burger-mobile. He is wearing an American flag bandana.

"Hey Barbie, sorry, didn't mean that. Didn't know it was you." As he approaches, turning shades redder with each step, I see no peaceful resolution on this horizon and try to close my window.

He catches it, slamming on the window. "You no good, first-generation, never gonna make it, off the boat…"

"Not true, Barbie," I plead, rolling the window shut over his hands.

"Ow! Open the window!" he pleads.

I retort, trying to leave quickly, "I'm American—about as American as hamburgers and french fries."

I squeeze the window shut over Barbaros' incredibly girthy exploding fingertips. "Later Alligator."

The television turns off. The lights turn off. Jaffar sticks his big face in mine illuminated by spinning police lights. "Yo, we gotta split, there's some beef going on," he says as he shakes me with obsessive force.

"Stop shaking me. I'm right here. Where's the beef?"

Jonas is now by the window cupping his ears. "Fuck no! Fuck no! Not a good trip, not a good trip." I jump off the sofa hearing police sirens spinning around me and feeling the insta-stress magnified around a million percent. Police cars are in the courtyard surrounding a pool of blood. "Is that blood?"

"Shhhhhhh! Shut your fuckin' piehole," Jonas whispers. "Get down or they'll see us." Jonas squats to the ground, pulling me with him. Jaffar shrinks into the corner. "I didn't do anything. I don't have anything. I'm gonna run, yeah, that's what I'll do..."

"Olivia was just down there with Keon. What the fuck's going on?" I ask a petrified Jonas who picks at the floorboards. "We're gonna have to dig our way underground," he says, lifting his head at me. I see his nose moving around his face, and his dreadlocks growing like living tentacles.

"Your hair is growing too fast!" I whisper, cringing away from several strands that threaten me.

"The portal is not up here." Jaffar beckons. "We have to get to the beach. Ioki will save us. This is a trap."

"Ioki? We're in a trap," I repeat, undoing the rubber band from my ponytail than redoing it until it snaps. "Shit. You're right, a trap." My hair falls across my face. I scream from my hair attacking me and leap back up.

"Shhhhhhh! What the fuck, Jehan!" Jonas blares at me, continuing to pick chicken scratches on the floorboards. I sneak one eye to the window. Xris is pegged against a police car screaming for bloody life, "Find that kid, he's up in the studio, I swear." Jaffar pushes me back down.

"They're gonna come up now. You shouldn't have looked."

"What's going on?" I can feel my heartbeat increasing as a paranoid darkness begins to smother my trip.

Jonas grabs my head, looking at me directly in the eyes. "You are not going to have a bad trip." His eyes glisten and vibrate with a blue aura that pushes the darkness back—for a second. "Listen to me. We are going to get the fuck out of here and find Ioki and the portal. Just relax."

I nod in anxious agreement as the sounds of Xris yelling continue: "The kid had it coming! I swear, go find what's-his-face! He'll tell you everything."

I hear a tremendous thud below us. It magnifies above us like a monster and is pounding on the ceiling. Jonas releases me as Jaffar stays stoic, head turning spasmodically towards the direction of the random thuds. Police lights flash in and out of the room.

"They are trying to get into the chamber. Hurry up, there is no time." Jonas opens the rickety wooden door.

Jaffar grabs me, stuck in a confused delirium. "Don't just stand there."

We make a dash down the spiral staircase. I hear thuds everywhere, the commanding voices of police officers through the walls, muffled instructions from the boys leading me down. "I'm about to vomit," I say as we near the exit. The three of us are huddled in front of the thumping door.

Jaffar looks at me and Jonas. "We're gonna bust this open and make a dash for the beach. Take the rear exit and if we get split up meet up at Beach 116th by the lifeguard benches."

I start to feel my stomach about to come up and hold my mouth. "I'm tripping balls," I gasp.

"Is anyone in there? Open up," the police shout through the door.

"One, two," Jaffar counts.

Jonas yells, "Three!" and kicks the door open to the spectacle of flashing lights behind silhouettes of what appear to be an army of police officers. My stomach rumbles as I try to follow the boys, but they vanish around the corner as quick as they bashed the door down. An officer grabs me, Xris yelling from the distance, "That's him!"

"Okay son, calm down, we just have to ask you a couple of—"

Then it all comes up. The world spins in circles as the mushroom puke shoots out of my mouth all over the cop as if God slowed time down. An eternity of pink liquid coats the officer's face and body. "Oh for fuck's sake!" he remarks, letting go of my arm.

I keel over and take a breath. "Can't talk… now, later alligator…" and take off around the bend.

Psychedelic mushrooms, known to the scientific community as *Amanita muscaria*, is a vomit drug. It doesn't give you euphoria. It doesn't make you feel "high" like your bottom barrel street drugs do. That's not the point of mushrooms. You will vomit, then the circles start. Some say ancient shamans manifest to spin the thoughts in your head into these definite shape-shifting things that are within spinning concentric circles. If you're a mess, the circles are a mess, however if you ride it out and let it crystallize, then the experience is nothing short of remarkable, and you walk away with an invisible token of your journey. Indeed, that explains why the three of us were writhing in sand looking up at the Rockaway night sky.

The Great Inaudible Hum

"I get it now," I say, lying horizontal on the beach.

"Space is a city of candles," Jaffar observes while covering himself in handfuls of sand.

Jonas begins singing, "All of us are with wings! All of us are with wings!" The night was about to break.

I inhaled the ocean waves with closed eyes, feeling the coolness of waves in my veins, resonating through my body, into my fingertips. "...resonating through my body," I say.

"You're into some good stuff," a voice replies. I open my eyes to a resonant presence standing beside me holding a metal detector over my face. The inaudible hum of the device sends a quiet blip to its master.

"All matter is resonating light," it says. The images of my past few months spin like slides in a view-master around the base of the device. "All... matter... is... resonating... light—vibrating at frequencies that bind it together."

"Welcome to the cipher, Ioki," Jaffar calmly pronounces.

"Wow," I react.

He continues, "You see, now you're outside of the pattern, looking down at the cycle. Now you can zoom above it and see the pattern of the cycle itself."

The images move in three hundred and sixty degree loops. As I focus on them, they form one circular, colorful thread. Just as I caught focus—"the violence, the music, the broken guitar, the slabs…"—they would shrink into an illuminated center.

"You see, all gone, right?" Outside of that compressed thread, a new set of images would form and do the same thing.

"It's getting faster and faster," I say.

Jonas comes over, "One must eat the other. Just zoom out, bro."

Jaffar, now covered in sand up to his neck, "It's like slapping yourself in the face! Wooooooo!" His howl echoed across every brick and concrete obstacle on the island.

"If you'd like to jump in the water, feel free," Ioki says. He moves the metal detector. Strands of his industrial strength wiry beard cover his white t-shirt with an imprint of a bunny rabbit.

"Feel free to be free of the freedom you feel," is placed in my ear.

I examined Ioki deeply. A mess of wires came out of his cheeks, entangled in the resonant frequencies around him: long strands of hair out of his chin, thin nose, a po-mo Confucius.

"I think I'll do that," I say, pushing myself up and inhaling the pure air of the Rockaway dawn as I dive into the Atlantic.

Behind me Ioki declares:

Prison'd on watr'ty shore
Starry Jealously does keep my den
Cold and hoar,
Weeping o'er,
I hear the father of the ancient men.

Bubbles and foam—blue speckles of light—the taste of ocean's salt—the sound of the oncoming storm. I made pacts with the Allies, had secret councils with the reef, and my whole body immersed in the sea for what was infinity. When I arose, the sun also appeared behind Olivia, who stood close by shuddering from the wind.

"Hey Sexy!" Olivia shouted as drips rolled off my skin.

"What brings you here?" I say.

"A little bird told me you and the boys would be tripping on the beach.

So how was it?"

I fall beside her. "It," I pause, "is not the trip but the vibrations—the beard man."

She gazes at me, laughing, "You are totally fucked up, Jehan."

"No, you're the fucked up one—in the darkness of the blood Church?" I say.

"Okay, that wasn't a sentence, but I'm going to assume that's trip talk for the beef last night? My brother got thrown in jail with Keon."

I rolled on my back, eyes wide open, licking the salt from my lips. "Beef and blood. The Rasta, you were talking to him as if—"

"I came here to tell you, we're all on the roof," she dusts sand off her ripped camo shorts and hops up, looking over me. "Everyone had a long night but now it's all just fine and dandy. Xris fucked that kid up pretty bad. You coming, or do you plan on cracking open more doors of perception?"

With a blink and an odd come-down feeling, we walked back to the Church. Where blood and cops stood the night before, there were crows and beer cans.

"I got it all figured out, down pat. I know what to do now. It's fucking crystal clear, Olivia, things are gonna be better. What time is it?" I ask.

"Good for you. It's around 8:30, Jehan, September 11th. Rise and shine!" She climbs the rusty ladder to the roof.

Although I watched the sun come up, the shaft of light shooting down the hatch blinded me. I put one hand over another, carefully lifting myself onto the tar roof. Olivia, Jonas, and Jaffar sat towards the Manhattan skyline hugging their knees. I joined them. "Aloha," I greet.

Jaffar, whose face is still covered in sand, is entranced.

Jonas briefly looks at me, then back out at the city skyline. "Ioki's a trip," he says. The effects of the mushrooms are subsiding, but in the daylight, the motion trails are accentuated.

"Dude, I'm re-inspired," I say.

Jaffar wiggles his fingers in my face, his fingers entering me through my chest and warping my posture like windmill slices. He laughs as I contort in rhythm.

"Chill, man," I plead. His fingers are synchronized to the sound of some infernal machine getting louder and louder. His mouth moves but the sound overshadows him—like an inaudible hum that makes all things around it silent. All of us look up to the heavens.

A passenger plane, flying low to the ground blasts above us, covering the sun and darkening the ground with its shadow. I see my friend's mouths moving, but am overwhelmed by the sonic vibrations of the engine and titanic motion trails happening above me. I freeze into a paralytic zone of over-stimulation; my eyes deadlocked wide open. Jaffar's hood goes flying off his head. My heart begins to race again as a harsh backdraft from the plane blows through us. The whole trip is sucked up with the plane's momentum as it darts towards Manhattan.

I lean into Jonas. "Yo man, I think I know what the next song is gonna be. Something about falling planes." Olivia jumps to action, the only one of us conscious enough to realize something is wrong.

"Holy shit!" she shouts.

Jaffar tells her, "That's perfectly normal, we're on the track, JFK Airport is right next to Rockaway." The plane gets more distant but does not gain altitude.

Jonas turns to me, "Falling planes, kid? Where did you come up with that idea?"

"I don't know, it just came—"

And then it happened...

A sonic boom across the water left all theories to haze sending us reeling back and gripping the tar below us. A smoke plume steadily formed out of the Twin Towers increasing in scale from second to second, and we sat there motionless on the roof of the Abandoned Church witnessing the distant silhouette of the Twin Towers go up in smoke and eventually down in flames. It was surreal, all happening miles away but clear as day from the Rockaway roof. I felt a pinch on my tongue as the second plane zoomed across, the last remaining shard of a broken tooth falling out of my mouth.

For two hours we said nothing and thought nothing. It felt like we were the only ones who knew until I heard in the streets below, "We gonna git those Arab fuckers!" I looked down the side for the source of the voice. The Russian crackhead Raymond Zakuska was pushing a cart with the studio computer and my television on it, images of the smoky towers playing through interference.

He looks up at me, "Is this all you had?"

Smoke & Mirrors

"That's it. I can't deal with this hair," Jonas said as we passed O'Hoolihan's Bar, a twenty-four hour Guinness tap for the local wombats. A bar filled with the old Rockaway Irish watched the television looping images of the collapse. One second they were up, next second they were falling. One second they were up, next second they were falling. Olivia pulled me away, "C'mon, let's go, everything is exploding."

"As soon as we get inside, I'm shaving these locks off," Jonas rambled, fidgeting with his sandy hair.

Jaffar lagged behind tempted by the scent of fresh alcohol. "I need a beer," he shouted taking something out of his pocket and throwing it at me. "Jehan, take my cell phone! I'll call you to get directions later." His dirty, cracked screen and beaten-up Nokia landed in my hands.

"Come on, come on," Olivia pestered. A woman, dressed for work, wandered aimlessly down the side of the road, suitcase in hand.

"You alright, lady?" I ask as we pass her. Splatters of dried blood on her face reveal through a layer of white powder all over her body.

"It's friggin' *Dawn of the Dead*, dude, look at that cloud." Jonas whispered in my ear.

The woman stopped briefly to gaze at the growing smoke cloud over the horizon, saying, "All exits in and out are shut down. Please exit the island. All exits are shutdown..."

We head towards Olivia's house.

"Hey lady, you should really get yourself to the hospital—"

Olivia pulled me away. "Stop tripping already! There's nobody there! Come the hell on!"

Olivia's place was a rickety one-family house stuck in between a gas station and the Far Rockaway low-income housing projects. "Last house on the left?" I conclude as the three of us enter through her squeaky front door.

"Wait here," she says, clearing off mounds of junk from the living room sofa. "I have to make sure my dad ain't around."

Jonas rushes to turn the television on, every channel showing the image loops of powdercoated people and the falling towers. "You think she would mind if I used her bathroom?" he asks me, doing my best to avoid looking at the television and not speaking. "Okay, whatever," the crusty mumbles as he disappears into the next room. On the television, repeating images of the falling towers intercut with shots of (supposed) Palestinians celebrating. I find it odd.

"Hey O!" I holler from the hallway. The walls are sparse except for photos of the family in better days. A marriage photo of Malachy and his wife, young Xris and his sister dressed like Buck Rogers and Princess Leia for Halloween, and an oddly wrinkled black and white photo with all of them— her mom's face scratched out.

"The coast is clear. I'm in here," she beckons. Her room had records sprawled all over the floor. "Well, this is it. You finally get to see my room."

"That's a high bed. How does a little girl like you reach it," I say, leaping onto what seemed a twenty-foot climb to the mattress. "You probably want to pass out—well, now is the time. My dad will throw a shit fit if he sees you guys are here. Do you have a place to crash tonight?"

"Eh, I'll find a place. I always do." I brush off the thought of sleeping while observing strips of bacon stapled on her wall to form the shape of a cross. "Is that actual bacon?"

"Damn, my Crass record is scratched. Oh well—what? Oh, that..." she finishes piling her records. "That was an art project I did in school. I call it *The Swingline Sacrilege*. Do you approve?"

"That seems like a viable name for such an unholy alliance of swine and office supplies. I can't imagine your dad appreciates it."

"Yeah, my dad usually just sits at his computer all day writing angry emails and plotting to kill tree-huggers." The sound of a buzzer hums on in the distance, the air becoming increasingly smoky. "Damn it," she slams the window closed.

I scroll through Jaffar's cell phone numbers. I recognize most of the names. "Religious food in the form of non-religious food is my specialty, so you've found the perfect guy."

"Yeah, right. I'm still waiting to figure out exactly who you are."

Jonas sits shirtless in Olivia's tub, covered with the pieces of his rambunctious hair, buzzing the last bits off. With no regard for cleaning up the disaster, he jumps out and flings his body in front of the mirror. "You lookin' at me, Rasta?" He flinches at himself. "Damn straight, you best not be looking at me." He glories in his newfound baldness. "Hold up—what you just say? Huh? Oh you're Arab? What?"

Malachy pushes the bathroom door open just as Jonas admires his overflexed jaw muscle.

"Uh oh." Jonas decrees, aghast.

Malachy scans the newly converted barbershop, and fumes in rage, grappling with the young man. "What is this? Does this look like a goddamn homeless shelter? You little scumbucket!"

I soothe Olivia, running my hands through her hair. "Fuck, Jehan, my dad!"

This was our last moment of calmness before Jonas screams in the background, "Get off me!"

Malachy storms into Olivia's room with Jonas in a headlock. "Today is not the day. Olivia! Oh look at what we have here."

His eyes widened as I pushed her head off my lap and lifted myself off the bed. "I was just leaving. No need to make a fuss, old man."

"A fuss? Now why would I make a fuss? Your people are the ones making a fuss and now you're all gonna pay!" Jonas struggled to get out of the fat man's grip.

"My people? You don't even know me dude."

"Oh I know you. You goddamn camel jockey Mooslems think you can just—"

"Dad, shut up," Olivia cried. "He's not Muslim! He's Irish and drinks and does drugs!"

"Oh thanks, O, big help you are. You forgot I also took your virginity." Malachy busts an artery. "All of you, get the hell out of my house!"

Jonas takes a deep bite into the man's arm and runs off. Malachy screams bloody murder, hitting the ground like a hungry giant.

Before I escape this *Island of Dr. Moreau*, I give Olivia a peck on the cheek and tell her the Allah honest truth: "Babes, I hate to break it to you, but I think I am Muslim."

Red September

In Brooklyn, you learn very quickly that your little national or foreign identity is not the center of the universe. You don't own this rock or even a little piece of this rock. You're just passing through. Passing through a place where tons of previous immigrants pulled their weight around, suffering through their own prejudices, their own battles, and their own distractions. For Italians, the distraction is whether you're Sicilian or Neapolitan. Big family battles exist on both sides. One side claims better pizza while the other claims better mafia. Even the nationalities known for their unity have problems within their little spheres. As much as it sounds absurd, 9/11 provided a much-needed aspirin from this. Everybody was given carte blanche to just hate one group: Muslim-kind. As Henry Rollins puts it, "Nothing brings people together more than mutual hatred."

"Vagrants and vagabonds, your attention please," Ms. Lolo shouted from the crooked crucifix in the Church courtyard. I rose up out of my sleeping bag to a scattered bunch of regulars, wiping the crust from my sockets. "Now I know you're all probably in deep mourning over what happened today," she continues holding up a newspaper with the headline: LIVE IMAGES MAKE VIEWER WITNESSES TO HORROR. Her Betty Page wig and floral dress are pristine.

I dig through my pockets and check Jaffar's phone—still no calls. A kid we call Fink stands next to me. "Hey, you see Jaffar around?" I ask him.

He nods negatively and points to his mouth showing me his ripped tongue. He's mute.

"Thanks, buddy. I know a tongue doctor in Swahililville—should get that looked at." Olivia stands by a looted beer barrel. "Hey, everything okay with your dad?" I ask her.

She turns her back to me.

"I'll take that as a no."

Lolo continues, "...but stealing the Church's sound equipment and computer is totally out of line. The Homeless Boys & Girls Club of Far Rockaway was set up to provide modern facilities to those in need, and this is just horrible!" With this statement, the crucifix falls apart.

Olivia turns to me, looking like a dog bit her ass. "I knew it. You're one of *them*!"

"Oh, get the fuck over it. Why don't you tell Lolo that Raymond took the stuff?" I feel sicker and sicker.

"You lied to me."

"No I didn't. You're watching too much TV or listening to your dad, whatever.""

If anyone knows anything about the whereabouts of my water buffalo head, or any of the other stolen items, please..." Ms. Lolo pleads in the background.

I shout, "It was Raymond and his Russian crackhead friends!" The crew wakes up from their unsympathetic circle. "I was on the roof this morning and I saw them taking off with everything in shopping carts."

Raymond Zakuska, a pear shaped Muscovite, wobbles up to Ms. Holo and angrily denies the charge. His mangled English accent juxtaposed with his emaciated junkie pervert look did not aid in his legal defense. "This is nonsense. He is one who probably stole them," pointing to me.

"Now why the hell would I steal anything from a place that's given me a place to sleep and work from? And where would I put it? Oh! Maybe, I can put them where I sleep and work!"

Ms. Holo panders to the rest of the courtyard. "In light of these astounding revelations, can anyone support Jehan's claim that these highly productive members of the Church..." The Russians fall back asleep, a syringe dangling off Vlad Blatt's arm. "...would dare steal anything? Remember, the Subvert Illuminatus knows the truth, so speak up!"

"Olivia was there with me. Tell Lolo what you saw." I plead to her.

Raymond groaned. Olivia stared desperately at me, then at Ms. Holo. As far as she was concerned, I killed everyone in the Towers, I put her brother in jail, and I was the poison to the Church's cynical merriment. Lolo checked her watch. "I ain't got all day sweetie. The Queens of Flatbush are holding a candlelight vigil in an hour, so what do you know?"

"He's a secret Moos'lem," she blurts out, covering her mouth immediately thereafter.

"Oh for fuck's sake!" I say. The voices of the Church begin whispering. A group of 8-year-olds with skateboards, known as The Children of the Torn, charted a quick way to torture me with hemorrhoid cream.

"Sweetie, what's his religious affiliation got to do with the location of my water buffalo head?"

The Church pit bull, channeling the pain of the invisible chains being wrapped around my neck, gave the canine equivalent of a shrug, lost interest, and began barking at a menacing figure that was walking in. A man with the head of a water buffalo and body of—hold on.

"Is this what you were looking for?" Xris removed the head from his body. "It was in the garbage outside."

"You're out of jail!" Olivia greeted him as the head crashed to the floor.

"Just the man I was looking for." Xris slowly circled me. "You could've prevented me from spending the night in jail and explained to the cops—"

"Dude, relax, I was tripping last night. Didn't you see the vomit?"

"Oh I saw it, and I saw you take off running like a little bitch." He shoved his mushed brawler face in mine. "And then I come home and my dad tells me the whole story. You and my sister—"

"You don't know the whole story dude, relax. Can we talk about this over paninis or something?" He wasn't enticed by my offer and whipped out a hunter's knife from his back pocket.

"Xris, you are out of line. Put that weapon away," Ms. Holo decreed.

The vibes get tense. He grabbed my throat with one hand, pinning me against the brick wall. I gasped for breath, suffocating as the brute held the knife to my jugular, windpipe in his grip. I was choking. Xris, the mixed up gone amok jarhead Nazi with one tour of duty in Browntown, personally showed me his colors don't run.

"I swear to God. I'll cut your throat, you little shit!" he yelled menacingly.

The Russians cheered him on. "*Priviet!*"

Olivia stood beside us. I noticed a slash across her right cheek. I could only imagine Malachy placed it there earlier. She urged him to cut my throat, "He's a terrorist!"

The secret was obviously out. I stared into the eyes of a man filled with hours of misinformation. Ms. Holo screamed, "You can't blame him for what happened and definitely not all of Muslim-kind. Xris, let him go." Lolo's pronouncement, mixed with Olivia's taunts, made this experience not go over so hunky-dory.

"You fucking towel-headed fag," he yelled again, beads of sweat coming down his wrinkled forehead.

I used my remaining breath to cough out, "You're thinking of Sikhs, Xris—they're the towel heads. I'm a—sandnigger from Texas—if anything." He stepped into me more as I choked out, "But since I'm white, I wouldn't exactly use the term nig..."

I was at the threshold of passing out. I wanted him to cut my throat and end the drama of explaining myself away to every angry person around me. First of all, I was not a practicing Muslim, and secondly, it seemed that everybody had turned into a racist overnight. Really, really bad racists too, which to me meant they had it in them in the first place and were just buttoned up about it. Grasping at straws, I didn't trust anyone anymore, so my death was a viable option.

He couldn't hold the anger and started crying, dropping the knife, falling on his knees, and sobbing in front of me. Olivia was confused.

"What the fuck, Xris! Don't start this shit again," she lectured him. Ms. Holo raced to the fallen weapon and discarded it. I fell to the ground, taking the biggest inhale ever.

For a second, I was upset that my nirvana would be canceled. I wanted to join with the resonant formless frequencies of the next life, but all I could summon up now was cracking my neck back into place.

"I can't do this," he said sobbing. "I don't want to go back."

I brushed myself off, taking a needed breather. Olivia stormed off insisting she never wanted to see either of us again. "You're a pussy, Xris. You'll always be a pussy. That's why they discharged you!"

Then she turned to me. "You should just change your name," Olivia spat out. "You'll have a much easier time. Plus no one can pronounce your name anyway!"

Ms. Holo joined in the identity conference, speaking directly at Olivia, "Jihad McBaconface is a fine name. He should keep his name the way it is. Get outta here, O! Now's not the time for your feedback."

"Olivia, do us both a favor and go back to Daddy. Blah. Blah." I respond.

"Fuck off, Jihad," she shouts, storming off.

"Okay people," Ms. Holo picks up her water buffalo head, "I have a vigil to go to. Everyone go back to your respective shanties and squats. This issue is over. Raymond, if the rest of the equipment is not on the property by tomorrow, consider this whole operation shut down. I have no time to teach a bunch of godless communists the meaning of punk rock ethics! Be happy this country even allowed you in with your Soviet 'rob-and-deny' bullshit."

As she walked off, Raymond hocked a massive loogie and spit near Ms. Holo's high heels. "American fuck," he said.

I massaged my neck and took some breaths, watching Xris breaking apart at the seams. "Go back where, dude?"

"The suck," he said. "I can just feel it, man. Bush is gonna send us back to finish off his daddy's shit."

"You mean the Middle East. I doubt we're going to war, man."

He lifted himself up, wiping his tears and eyeing the Russian junkies. "Oh there's evidence, kid. You've been sleeping all day. We got passports, footage, and last I heard, their ringleader, Oshama Ben something or other, delivered a message to the press."

"If you have to go fight," I told him, "do it and do it one hundred percent. I bet you'll find some real terrorists somewhere out there, beneath the crescent moon." The Disney logo glistened over my teeth.

Xris spit at Raymond, "Get out of here, or you're gonna get what's coming to you." The Russians mumbled assorted curses in their native tongue as they slowly emptied out of the courtyard. Xris turned back to me. "You telling me to kill your people?"

"I don't have any people!" I responded. "Just a whole lot of questions."

He stretched out the same fist he choked me with. " I didn't mean to hurt you. Shit's getting complex."

I slammed his fist in unity and said, "And I didn't mean to hurt you—by existing."

Town Runnin' Dry

My hair grew an inch in a week and although the air still smelled of the burning towers, there were no explosions, no destructions, only scanners. I exiled myself under the boardwalk, devising a slap-dashed attempt at suicide that I hoped would make me famous.

Headline:

Muslim Rocker Kills Self After 9-11, Leaves Note Saying Sorry for Being Quasi-Brown and Born Moozle. Salami Legume, Jihad McBaconface.

A window shade near my boardwalk cubbyhole was lifted, the bright light bringing me back to consciousness from the plastic bag I was suffocating myself in. I could not bear outing myself this way and poked holes in the nostrils just as things got deep. I glanced towards the light, seeing only the backs of a family illuminated by their television light. Their eyes targeted on the scrolling news flashes just like a million silent stares through a sniper rifle.

And their orders were coming in loud and clear. A little girl pulled down the shade. I took the bag off my head, hearing the cling-clanging of high heels above. I had written a suicide note and placed it in Lolo's mailbox earlier in the day. It read:

To those that come after me, whom I will not have the grace of meeting in person, the world is a cruel place. It should come as no surprise that due to unforeseen circumstances I would have to commit suicide in such a poor way. If I had loot, Doctor Kevorkian would be on the first red-eye but alas a plastic bag will have to do.

I didn't do it! Sorry muthaflowas!

I could see through the ripped bag up her skirt at her dangling package. "Ew," I said.

She yelled through the boardwalk, "For someone who thinks they're so smart, you act like a zombie perv! Get the hell up here, Jihad. I don't have all day!"

Lolo dug through her oversized green purse smelling of chewing gum and lipstick. The shore was empty.

"Bad days, Ms. Holio," I groaned, tossing the torn bag away.

"It's Holo, I'm not a friggin' candy snack! I got nothing for you, Jihad. It's you and a dozen other kids with no place to squat. The Church is kaput, el sinko like el Titanico." She pulled in the collars of her wool coat and popped his/her lips as a cold wind rushed through my body.

"Wake up, Jihad. It's not because you're an orphan... or whatever you say you are. You're the only Muslim on the whole island. That's why you're hanging out with me, that's why your little white girlfriend dumped you, and that's how shit's gonna go for years. Get used to it."

My eyes were wide open.

She continued, "You're the modern fag—oppressed and undressed."

When an old drag queen shouts at a person whose last meal was a blend of psychoactive mushrooms and beer, assume that person could care less if he drown or froze.

"Is that it?" I asked as she defiantly stood up, gathering herself to return to her new role as media scanner. "What happened to hearts for the heartless?"

Lolo swooped her scarf over her shoulder. "You're a shape shifter, Jehan, but you have a heart—go shape shift. You'll be fine."

The neon pink and green logo for Stamos & Blaunstein Productions flashes as a scene dissolves of a post-apocalyptic war zone. "In a world of good and evil," a raspy narrator exclaims, "where evil lives in a place where good is doing its damnedest to spread their awesome goodness..."

We see the back of an enormous soldier for the Greater Bright Zone taking a Hot Pocket out of a toaster and feed it to a starving brown child in rags. The child look up and says, "tanks meesta—maybe one day I'll be big and strong like you." The camera follows the soldier's hand to his face—it's Arnold Schwarzenegger.

"Keep eating your food, kid. Let Jesus into your heart and learn to exfoliate."

The ceiling caves in and paratroopers dressed in yellow turbans yelling, "Gooba! Gooba! Gooba!" drop in.

The voice starts up again. "One man is called upon to kick some ass and smoke the evil do'ers out of their holes!"

Arnold flips out two semi-automatic laser photon blasters for each hand and incomprehensibly yells, "Why do you hate us!?"

The turban wearing mystery men look at each other, dumbfounded that they've upgraded their acting roles from playing hijackers to playing paratrooping terrorists. One guy says to the other, "I considered not taking this role, but I figured what the hell. I was sick of playing Puerto Ricans on *Law & Order*."

The other guy responds in full flaming diva-speak, "Hold up, I'm Puerto Rican—*Boricua ho!* —and I'm sick of playing Arabs on *Law & Order*."

Yet another paratrooper hesitantly drops his AK-47 and pulls out a long scroll that he opens. "I can read you quite a long list of reasons of why we hate you. Let's start with #452, also known as the Lost Battle of Vienna..."

Arnold a.k.a. Lenny, vigilante mercenary for the Greater Bright Zone's Operation: Target Everyone campaign, grinds his teeth and tells the men, "This is for freedom, the investors that financed this movie, and the street cred I continue to receive for killing brown people played by a mélange of ethnicities." He fires his guns, taking the kid's arm right off and missing most of the paratroopers.

"You asked for it!" he screams.

The Puerto Rican turns to the camera. "Black Sambo is alive and well in 2001!" His final eulogy is followed by his body decimated from Arnie Big Gun's photon destroyers.

The voice continues, "Arnold is back, and this time he is taking no I—O—U's because" (dramatic pause as the title of the movie zooms in from the onscreen explosions) "Schmerman Morplanx's *The Check's in the Mail* (video game coming soon for Popstation 2 and F-Box)."

As the sky continues to fall I look up at a billboard for *Collateral Damage*, with Arnold in it. Next to his big fat face are the words, "Veteran Firefighter's

Wife and Child Killed in Bomb Blast. What would you do if you lost every-thing? SCHWARZENEGGER, *COLLATERAL DAMAGE.*

"The irony is thicker than the falling asbestos," I thought on my way to work. Everything seemed to be on its side. I was realizing things were set up a certain way. I passed the deli on Beach 116th Street. A headline from the *Post* blared out: ANTI-ARAB ASSAULTS SURGE HERE. As I flipped through, reading what amounted to a modern day call for race-war, I noticed another rack beside the newspapers. Out of place and oddly arranged, it was a stack of homemade Xeroxed brochures that turned out to be infinitely more depressing.

The front page had a picture of the deli I was in front of with high im-pact font that read: **Halal Bakery haven for terrorists. Watch out residents!!**

I picked one up and opened it, revealing a large block of text:

The local seemingly harmless looking deli/bakery/cabbie hangout on the corner is actually a secret cell for terrorists plotting their next moves. Protect your children! Hide your treasures! And most of all, hold your Bible tight! They are among us!

Rockaway Freedom Minister, Doctor Malachy.

"Good to see someone is keeping themselves busy," I said out loud, growing more dejected and tossing the propaganda into the next available trash bin. The sense of confusion and loss of self didn't matter much. At least I had a job—that is, until I turned the corner.

Kaffir Beurger, with Barbaros' large pig wearing a kufi sign, had been burned down. The sign dangled from its post emblazoned with poorly worded graffiti over it: "Kafir PiG!"

Again, the double irony seemed thick. The windows were smashed; the seats now blackened crisps of foam and burned vinyl, white and hot sauce containers. The grill and the floors were coated with water, and all the van-dals could come up with was the name of the place. I entered through the bashed-in door, my Converse cracking ashy carbon bits with each step. The doorbell still rang though as I entered. "Hello?" I shouted, hearing the sound of a spoon hitting the soup cauldron in the back.

The menu on the wall, once offering a special Kaffir Beurger with Hummus now said, "Turk FuK, eat pig Die!" Again, they missed the irony— we didn't serve pig.

"I'm a hamburgers and french fry kid like every other American kid" wandered through my mind. I looked at the grill and remembered Mr. Hogzilla and his band of fake pork slabs that would sing me glam rock songs. Poor guys. Barbaros stood in the still smoking kitchen, frozen over the tarred cauldron filled with water and burned chunks of sheetrock.

"*Merhaba*, Barbie," I greeted. His eyes glazed over with tears, spinning the ladle repeatedly as if there was work to be done.

"You're ten minutes late, Jehan. We need peppers and onions. You look awful."

"Thanks... but... I'm not really here..." I narrowly avoided a falling piece of lumber.

"I worked my whole life for this place," he said, his lips quivering. "It was always about service, customer service. I learned back in Istanbul, the customer is always right. Always right. Didn't I teach you that all the time, right?"

"Yes, you did, Barbie. Who did this?"

"You know, when the Turks ruled the Arabs we never had a problem with them. When the Ottomans ran the Caliphate we brought Europe out of the Middle Ages. Took the ignorant alchemy and made it chemistry, we had soap while England died of plague from their dirty ways..."

"And now," I said.

"And now, look at where we are. Arabs did this. The secret 9/11 operation to burn bridges—you believe this. This was my store!"

"So Muslims burned down a Muslim business? I thought everything was..."

"Yes, yes—the *Talifoondies*. They have been on my back since we opened. They hate Turks. British mind-control. I was trying to build bridges with the food, and now they've destroyed!"

"Yes, the tofu and chickpea korma was very progressive." I nodded, backing away as he poured an illimitable Turkish melancholia into the hallucination of lentil soup. "Well, I'm gonna split, Barbie. Better that I move on anyway. Hey, you got my last week's pay?"

He looked up at me. "Wear the hat one more time, would you? Just say welcome to Kaffir Buerger. May I help you? One more time, and I'll give you your pay."

I couldn't refuse the poor old guy or the dough. The rubber floppy pig hat was in bad shape but still wearable in a Malcolm McLaren Sex Pistols sort of way. I shook the ashes off of it. The pig's face was contorted seven ways to hell and deep-fried from the blaze. I managed to get it on my head, and it flopped in the wrong direction as usual. Barbaros smiled, and I said it: "Welcome to Kaffir Beurger, where the pigs are figs and the sauce is holy."

"No," he said now, brighter than before, "the pigs are holy and the sauce is figs."

"You never had it right either, Barbie," I say, the front doorbell letting out a ring. "A customer," Barbaros wondered.

"Are you guys still open?" she said. The voice was familiar—comforting. I ran to see who it was. "I want to redeem my coupon, did it expire yet?" She asked as my inner floppy-sticky-octopus finalized its ascent. I walked into the light—an inner soundtrack from a bad romantic comedy started. I looked in her eyes and realized everything had led me to this point; the resonant frequencies, the circle of life, and all that stuff Ioki was talking about. Zoom out, zoom out.

"Dalya, right?"

"Jehan, right?" she smiled scandalously, her Jewish Star of David necklace shimmering in a ray of light. I squinted. The rest of her was the hottest snow bunny south of Alaska.

"Sorry, the only thing we're cooking today is Soup d'Ash." I realized that I was still wearing the hat and quickly took it off.

"Well I have a coupon, and I want to redeem it."

I remembered the better days now, when the world was still okay. I had written a little note to her. She handed it back. I opened it:

Jehan (happy face) You're my new muse, use this for a free Nutshake, Come again (picture of pig with a kufi)

"My nutshake brings all the girls to the yards." I nod knowingly.

Barbaros came out with his ladle. "Is everything alright Jehan?"

Dalya grabbed me and pulled me out. "Let's get busy, nutter!"

I turned back to Barbie, "Yeah, I'm just building bridges. Salami Legume!"

ABOUT THE AUTHOR

Cihan Kaan is a Texas-born, Brooklyn-raised writer and filmmaker. His short film *She's Got an Atomic Bomb* (2004) won Best Short Film for the Evil City Festival and toured underground film festivals such as the Coney Island Film Festival, the B-Movie Film Festival (winner of the Audience Award), and the Lost Film Festival.